KILLING FROST

KILLING FROST

A Deets Shanahan Mystery

Ronald Tierney

Severn House Large Print
London & New York

This first large print edition published 2016
in Great Britain and the USA by
SEVERN HOUSE PUBLISHERS LTD of
19 Cedar Road, Sutton, Surrey, England, SM2 5DA.
First world regular print edition published 2015 by
Severn House Publishers Ltd., London and New York.

British Library Cataloguing in Publication Data

Tierney, Ronald author.
    Killing frost. – (The Deets Shanahan mysteries)
    1. Shanahan, Deets (Fictitious character)–Fiction.
    2. Private investigators–Indiana–Indianapolis–
    Fiction. 3. Murder–Investigation–Indiana–
    Indianapolis–Fiction. 4. Detective and mystery stories.
    5. Large type books.
    I. Title II. Series
    813.5'4-dc23

    ISBN-13: 9780727870124

Severn House Publishers support the Forest Stewardship Council™
[FSC™], the leading international forest certification organisation. All
our titles that are printed on FSC certified paper carry the FSC logo.

Typeset by Palimpsest Book Production Ltd.,
Falkirk, Stirlingshire, Scotland.
Printed and bound in Great Britain by
T J International, Padstow, Cornwall.

To all the souls who have escaped or are about to

Acknowledgements

Killing Frost was made possible by all of the usual suspects, brothers Richard and Ryan, Jovanne Reilly and David Anderson.

25th Anniversary Appreciation

On this 25th anniversary, thanks go to the readers, librarians and bookstore owners. I also want to thank family and friends for their support and encouragement, Ruth Cavin for giving me a start, Otto Penzler for providing a bridge to a new publisher when I needed one, and Severn House's Edwin Buckhalter for taking me in.

Author's Note

The Deets Shanahan books haven't broken any new ground in the mystery genre. However, from the beginning, Shanahan wasn't standard issue. He was old. He lived in a mid-sized city, one that didn't have the dangerous, exotic feel of New York, Los Angeles or San Francisco. I should note, though, there were other fictional private eyes of advanced age, and Indianapolis was home to Albert Sampson before Shanahan moved to the city's East Side. Sampson is the famous Indianapolis PI penned by Michael Z. Lewin, who is also credited with establishing the concept of regional mysteries. Lewin opened the door for many crime writers. Publishers, who lived and worked in New York, could be a little provincial. Someone had to break the rules so the rest of us had a chance. Shanahan was one of the lucky ones.

St Martin's Press held onto my first attempt at a mystery novel, *Stone Veil*. It was probably in a stack of papers in a dusty corner of the Flatiron Building for the two years before I finally called and asked whoever answered the phone to return it. The guy asked me to be patient. They had just hired a new editor and the voice was sure she would like it. The late, legendary Ruth Cavin liked it enough to publish it.

The book did well. It received an encouraging review from the *New York Times*, was nominated for a Shamus Award for Best First Novel from the Private Eye Writers of America (PWA) and was serialized in an Eastern European magazine. I might have preferred French, but I was happy as could be. There was, as it turned out, a significant Latvian population in Indianapolis who might have enjoyed it. Sadly, I had no idea my book had been nominated for a national prize. No one told me, so I was spared public defeat when Walter Mosley won the Shamus that year for *Devil in a Blue Dress*.

I have to confess, I had no idea what I was doing in those days. I knew very little about the genre. I was, of course, familiar with Hammett and Chandler, mostly through the movies. In fact, just about all my exposure to mysteries came through black-and-white double features when, as kids, my older brother and I spent weekends in the dark environs of the grand old movie houses in downtown Indianapolis. Later, I read *The Spy Who Came in From the Cold* and several books by Graham Greene, as well as all the very slim volumes of James Bond's adventures, but I had no idea how many great mystery writers would have enthralled me had I only known about them.

There was something forbidding about those tough, dangerous-looking paperbacks in the squeaky, swiveling metal stand in the drugstore. I had the sense that they were as forbidden as the little bottles of whiskey on the wall behind the cash register. Unfortunately the pharmacist knew my mother, so my glances at the rack were fleeting. There was a history of the pharmacist and the barber and the grocer telling parents about their wayward children. I learned of their secret network and adapted.

It's probably still the case, PI books (pulp fiction) are rarely taught in high school or college literature courses. I remained uninformed until I decided, at forty-something, to start writing them. This separates me from many of my peers who write crime fiction and who were schooled in it much earlier in their lives. This ignorance on my part wasn't entirely negative. I was able to skip the new writers' mimic phase altogether, allowing me to find my own voice very early on. On the other hand, there is a valued tradition to uphold. And there was and is much to learn from veterans in the field.

One of the things I learned I could have only learned by doing. Just because a writer creates characters doesn't mean he or she can tell them what to do. When I created Maureen, I had no idea she would play such a meaningful role in every adventure. Although the books are called 'Deets Shanahan Mysteries,' Maureen is not a supporting player. As I got to know her, I realized she would never have permitted it. She is smart, funny and strong. A few readers have written me to suggest I knock off Shanahan and let her take over the business. I couldn't split them up. It is a genuine love affair that began in the first book. Though they never married, they became a team. I'm convinced that the series' success is based on the way they relate to each other.

The two of them have had harrowing adventures. They have had fun. So have I – from their odd and awkward meeting in *Stone Veil* to the political mystery, *Iron Glove*, the bizarre comedy of *Nickel-Plated Soul* and the scary and suspenseful mystery *Asphalt Moon* to this tough thriller, *Killing Frost*, and all the others.

The truth is I'm surprised and grateful for the durability of the series. Even so, I still feel like an interloper. There are so many great writers out there, many who started earlier, wrote more, sold more and are more highly regarded. Still, a quarter of a century for old Shanahan isn't bad, and I am pleased to present this particular story – *Killing Frost*. This is the eleventh and perhaps last book in the series. It is a little shorter than the others. However, I do not apologize. It is simply the way Shanahan told it.

We are getting late in his life. What I wanted to relate is a continuation of his character – dogged determination, eyes-wide-open loyalty and protector of those he loved and believed in – even as age, infirmity and overpowering danger threatens it.

One

Even a cautious sort plays the odds. We're all gamblers. We have to be. Cross the street, get hit by a car. Take a shower, slip in the tub. Have dinner in a restaurant and choke on a bone. The odds may vary. But every moment of existence is a gamble. All a guy has to do to flirt with death is just sit there, minding his own business. A vein can burst and it's all over in seconds.

Deets Shanahan sat in his usual chair in the living room, staring out of the window, waiting, thinking about death. It would have been welcomed not so long ago, before he met Maureen. Before she came into his life, he was a man who sat, night after night, on a stool in a dim bar that smelled of ammonia and urine, patiently waiting for death to overtake him.

Because of Maureen, living became a generally good way to pass the time. But lately, thoughts of death intruded as they did now while he waited for a knock on the door. Death could, he imagined, looking at his watch, come before the dreaded appointment with Mrs Alexandra Fournier. The odds in this case favored the arrival in his life of Fournier, a potential client and a woman not easily put off, though he had done his best to do so.

He looked again out the window. He closed his eyes. At seventy-two he embraced the notion that

1

he had a few more years left. However, it appeared his change of heart about checking out early wasn't necessarily shared by a contrarian universe.

After the tumor was removed from his brain and a second surgery to relieve the swelling and inflammation not only failed but cut into his motor nerves, he had decided to turn his retirement from semi to full. His left hand and arm were left somewhat unresponsive. Using his left hand like a claw, he could hook around or grip something like a flashlight in a rudimentary way, but couldn't turn a page in a magazine or pick up a penny off the floor. Or tie his shoes. He had a slight lurch to the left when he walked. It was a slow metamorphosis, he thought – turning into a crab – though he appreciated the humor in God's, or an indifferent universe's, choice of symbol.

Perhaps a demonstration would convince Mrs Fournier she should find a newer model of PI to handle her case, whatever that turned out to be. He checked his watch again, 11:06, went to the window and looked down the slope of his leaf-covered lawn. Sometimes it was difficult to find the house. There was a Pleasant Run North Drive and a South Drive, one on each side of a tree-and bush-lined creek. Though Shanahan lived on South Drive – on *East* South Drive to make things worse – he could see both streets from his window. No one seemed lost.

Mrs Fournier wouldn't say what she wanted on the phone. And he would have discouraged her even more firmly, except that she had been referred by Jennifer Bailey, an old friend of Shanahan's, a highly respected former Indiana state attorney general. The battered old PI had to at least hear the woman out.

When the phone rang, he was sure it was his client asking for directions or, he thought with sudden and uncharacteristic optimism, cancelling the whole affair.

It was Maureen.

'I have to show a home on the north side at six. Do you want me to pick up something for dinner or do you want to cook?'

'Those are my choices?' Shanahan asked.

'You can take me to dinner.'

He had to be careful. Going out to dinner involved serious negotiations. Maureen usually wanted to try the newest restaurant in town. That too often meant small portions of artfully placed but largely unrecognizable food, accompanied by a sizable check. Shanahan preferred the tried and true. He needed a plan.

'How about Sakura's?' he asked in as casual a tone as he could manufacture.

'Shanahan.' It wasn't quite a whine, but it was a tone that preceded a complaint. It was working. 'That means I'd have to go crosstown twice.'

'I could meet you there,' he said, again feeling the guilt. She didn't want him driving yet. There was a question about his field of vision since the surgery, not to mention the possibility of seizures. He felt bad about the deception, but not bad enough. He didn't want a fancy evening. He was exhausted already, and the day had barely begun.

'That's a lot of driving for you. Let's not push it.'

'Got it. How about Amici's?'

'OK,' she said, and after a pause added, 'but I think you just tricked me.'

'I've got to go,' Shanahan said, watching as a frail, elderly lady emerged from a well-maintained vintage Buick parked in his driveway. Her coat-tails flapped in the breeze as she placed her purse on the hood of the car and raised her hands to hold onto her hat.

Her body jerked. Her body went limp. Her hat blew away. She crumpled, dropping straight down onto the gravel below.

Two

Shanahan punched 911 and moved to the door. Outside was eerily quiet. He provided the operator with his location and a description of what he saw. The lady was face down. When he knelt to one side, he saw the blood trail, followed it to the hole in the back of the neck where it met the skull. Her silver hair matted at the bullet's entrance. He took her wrist, felt for a pulse, checked again under her chin. None. He answered 'yes' and 'no' to the operator's questions but saw no point in continuing the conversation.

'The name is Shanahan and I'll be here when the police arrive.' He disconnected, put the phone in his pocket as he stood. It registered. A bullet. He looked down the sloping yard to the stretch of green that divided the two parkways. He decided to get out of what was likely the line of fire, moving to the front of the Buick and grabbing her purse as he went. He wiped the straps with his handkerchief and opened it. He had only a few moments. He wasn't sure why he was doing this. Habit. Instinct. Yes, he did know. He was going to have to know what she wanted. The police weren't always helpful.

Depending on who showed up to investigate, homicide detectives could be more hostile than helpful. He rummaged through her purse.

Brush, compact, lipstick, wallet, pen, address

book. He found one of his old business cards, one with the old address. That address had been crossed out and above it the current one. Twenty-three dollars cash in the wallet and a driver's license issued to Alexandra Fournier, who lived in the Butler–Tarkington area of the city. There were also school photographs of children, all dressed up and smiling. Credit cards, supermarket discount cards. The content included what seemed like random sheets of paper. One turned out to be a grocery list. Another, written on a torn corner of a lined legal pad, had an address. Only an address. Same writing as the corrections on his business card.

He heard the sirens. Two kinds. Police and fire. He put the purse and its contents back where he found them. He kept his business card and the torn piece of paper.

The medics quickly lost interest in the body. Nothing they could do. The uniformed police appeared a little lost. Two conferred with the medics. When they were finished, the slender one approached Shanahan and the other was on the phone – to homicide, Shanahan thought.

'You called it in?' the young officer with MacGregor on his nametag asked.

'I did.'

'You want to talk me through it?'

Shanahan gave him an abbreviated version, knowing he'd be talking people through it a number of times before the afternoon was over.

'My guess is the shot came from down there.' Shanahan pointed to the parkway.

'A shot? You know it's a gunshot?'

6

'Pretty much.'

'You an expert on these things?'

'I'd take the medical examiner's word over mine, but I'd probably be checking out where the bullet likely came from . . .'

MacGregor looked unsure for a moment. Other uniforms were stretching out the yellow tape. MacGregor took a small notebook from his shirt pocket.

'I saw her fall, Officer. There was no one around. She was shot from behind and from a distance.'

'I have no idea why you called the police. You have it all figured out. You wouldn't happen to have him locked in a cell inside, would you?'

'Maybe we could just wait for homicide.'

The officer put his notebook in his shirt pocket, retrieved his cuffs and asked Shanahan to turn around. Shanahan felt the cool metal on his wrists, heard the click.

'Maybe you feel a little less in charge this way, Mr . . .?' He turned Shanahan back around so they were facing each other again.

'Shanahan. Ask away.'

'How do you know her?'

'I don't.'

'What was she doing here?'

'She thought maybe I could help her.'

'Help her in what way?'

'She didn't say.'

MacGregor called out to one of the officers, told him to search the house.

'Warrant?' Shanahan asked.

'Scene of the crime. Suspect right here.'

7

'You sure you don't want to wait for someone who knows about these things?'

The medical examiner arrived, looked around awhile before focusing on the body.

'Anything you want to tell us before we go in?' MacGregor asked. 'Maybe you have a firearm?'

'I do. A forty-five.'

'You have a permit.'

'Yes.'

'Fired recently?'

'No. And your victim was shot with a smaller caliber.'

'There you go again.'

Another big black four-door pulled up in front. There weren't that many homicide cops. Shanahan knew a few of them, including Lieutenant Swann, who plucked his suit jacket from the back seat and put it on as he walked up the slight hill. Shanahan felt better. Unless he'd changed more than the few extra pounds since he'd last seen him, this was a good sign. Swann was a by-the-book-cop. Sometimes frustrating, it was a reliable characteristic. The cop, on the other hand, wasn't surprised or particularly happy to see Shanahan.

Swann changed his route halfway to the front of Mrs Fournier's Buick, where MacGregor and Shanahan stood. The lieutenant spoke with the medical examiner. It was brief. Shanahan knew why. It wasn't complicated. Though a more complete examination would be made, it was likely the examiner, and now Swann, knew the cause of death and generally where the bullet came from. Swann picked up the woman's purse on his way.

'Would you tell Officer MacGregor that I won't hurt him?' Shanahan asked Swann, turning so the handcuffs would be visible.

Swann nodded. MacGregor, obviously unhappy, freed him.

'He was acting in a disrespectful manner,' MacGregor said.

'That *is* his manner,' Swann said. 'He's an acquired taste.'

'Kind of a dill pickle,' Shanahan said.

'Hold up there, guys,' Swann yelled at the uniforms headed for Shanahan's front door. 'Forget the house. Down the hill, straight down before you spread out both ways. Look for shell casings, .22 probably. Check for any signs of someone having settled in.' He pointed straight down, then looked at Shanahan. 'Small bullet, straight in. Judging by how she fell and the entrance angle of the bullet. The only way you could believe this was an accidental shooting by a squirrel hunter is to believe that you will win the lottery.'

Young MacGregor glanced at Shanahan, no doubt waiting for the 'I told you so.' Shanahan remained quiet.

'Get some help,' Swann said to MacGregor, 'and start talking to the neighbors. Put Fisher in charge of the weeds. I'll take Shanahan.'

MacGregor gave both of them a respectful nod.

Shanahan didn't mind making enemies, but it wasn't a goal.

Inside, Swann went to the fireplace, leaned against the mantlepiece to make a call. Shanahan was pretty sure he was calling the higher ups. Shanahan went to the kitchen to do the same.

'Maureen, do you have a few minutes you can squeeze into your schedule?'

'What do I get out of it?'

'A rum and tonic or a pint of pistachio gelato.'

'Strike the "or" in our contract.'

'I need information, as much as I can get on an Alexandra Fournier. Where she works or worked. Organizations she belonged to. Religion, politics, education, friends and family, favorite charities, passionate interests. Do your Google thing and fax back what you find.'

'Fax? We might still have a carrier pigeon around here somewhere.'

'I'm surprised you haven't eaten it.'

'That will cost you a bottle of good wine. Is there anything else I can put on your tab?'

'I've learned my lesson.'

'So she showed up? You have work?'

'I don't know how to answer that,' Shanahan said as Swann appeared in the doorway. 'Dinner is on, right?'

'Same lady?' Swann asked, nodding to the phone as Shanahan slid the phone into the charger.

'Very same.'

'Good,' Swann said. 'She's too good for you.'

'I try to keep that fact from her.'

They went back into the living room, where Shanahan explained what little information he had. He brought up Jennifer Bailey's name as a reference. That meant something to the lieutenant. Being the only woman to hold that office – and a black holding high political office in Indiana

10

at that – there was a certain celebrity associated with her name. She was also still active in public affairs and still respected, which meant she had a bit of power in the community as well. If she called a press conference, the media would show up.

She was also first on the list of people Shanahan wanted to talk to.

Swann excused himself and with phone in his hand stepped out onto the front porch. He wasn't gone but for a moment.

'Collins is on his way out.' Collins ran the Homicide Division, as far as Shanahan knew. But how the police department was organized was a mystery in itself. Swann was pretty high up. Collins was higher. The victim was likely important in some way. This wasn't the standard homicide unit.

The moment was awkward.

'Didn't you used to have a dog?' Swann asked.

'And a cat. Got old. Rough year.'

Swann nodded.

The house was quiet, suddenly hollow. Before he died, Shanahan's old Catahoula hound used to plunk down on the rug in front of the fireplace and Einstein the cat, who lived to be twenty, usually found the sunniest spot to nap. Sometimes, Shanahan thought he still saw them from time to time – a quick glance out of the corner of his eye.

'Guess I'll see what the boys are doing.' Swann looked uncomfortable. He went out front, stood in the middle of the front yard, perhaps on some level – personal, professional, cosmic – to make sense of it all.

11

Three

Swann and Collins couldn't be more different. Swann wore a suit because he had to. However, on him, it looked like an afterthought. Collins wore a suit because he liked to look good. That was how Shanahan interpreted the dowdy, plodding white cop and the stylish, energetic black one. Shanahan had worked with them both in the past. As far as cops went, Shanahan could've done worse. Swann was thorough. Collins had a quick, open mind.

'How is it you get involved in these things?' Collins asked. 'Are you the only fucking PI in the city?' He smiled at the universe. 'What are the odds?'

'You don't love me anymore?' Shanahan went to the window. He could see dozens of blue uniforms scurrying about below.

'I do, Shanahan. I do. But why you? Why always you?' He went to the sofa, held the creases to his crisply pressed pants as he sat. 'All right. Unless something pops out of the blue, this is the simplest, most straightforward crime scene I've ever come across. If we rule out accident, we've got a professional hit or a gunshot from a highly talented amateur. And then . . . that's it. A big, dark hole. By the way, Fournier, if you don't know already, is Jennifer Bailey's sister. So this' – Collins' arms spread wide – 'is the calm before the storm.'

12

Shanahan did know. Maureen's fax arrived while Swann was outside managing the swarm of uniforms before Collins arrived. Alexandra Fournier didn't have the celebrity of her sister, but she was no slouch in the power-behind-the-scenes department. She headed the task force for civilian oversight of the police force. She was the founder of an organization to help kids with juvenile crime backgrounds get educational grants. She was a member of the board of several charities involving children, animals and those otherwise dispossessed. Her husband, a judge, died five years ago of a heart attack. Shanahan didn't volunteer the information for two reasons. He wasn't sure he should get involved and he wasn't sure he'd be allowed to get involved. This was an active murder investigation. But he wanted in. He'd like to have their OK, even if it wasn't official.

Shanahan continued to look out of the window.

'You see a flash?' Collins asked.

'No. I wouldn't. Too bright outside.'

'Hear anything? A pop?'

Shanahan tapped the glass in the window. 'Double paned. Eco-friendly.'

'Penny pincher,' Collins said.

'Why am I part of your little gathering?' Shanahan asked. Swann looked at Collins, no doubt eager to get the answer as well.

'You are our only witness,' Collins said. 'It's more comfortable in here, even without your offer to make some coffee, than it is outside. And I know, as sure as I know Swann will object, that you won't be able to stay out of it.' Swann bowed his head and gave it a subtle shake of unhappy submission. 'You also have a relationship with Miss Bailey.'

'Not necessarily a good one. Coffee?' Shanahan asked, aware now that while Swann would still keep Shanahan at arm's length, Collins would bend the rules if need be.

'How thoughtful,' Collins said.

It was true what Maureen said. 'You want things the way they used to be.'

He couldn't and wouldn't argue. He didn't like computers or smart phones. He resented microwaves and electric can openers. He wouldn't use GPS or ATMs. The only modern, if you could call it that, convenience that gained his approval was the TV remote.

So, when it came to restaurants, the demise of so many of the regulars limited his choice. If it was to be Italian, the choice was easy for him. Iaria's or Amici's. Both had been around for a while, and both served simple bona fide Italian food: some sort of pasta and sauce. Certainly nothing hard to pronounce, though he'd have to admit Maureen had expanded his vocabulary with regard to menus of various ethnic origins.

He chose Amici's because they were cabbing it and Amici's was closer. It was almost too dark in the small, crowded dining room. Shanahan always thought this out-of-the-way place was a perfect rendezvous for cheating couples. With a beautiful, younger woman across from him, sipping deep red wine, he could imagine himself

14

in an illicit dalliance rather than with the well-established love of his life.

'Did you sell the house?' Shanahan asked. They didn't talk in the taxi.

'I'm getting an offer tomorrow.'

He started to say something suggestive, but backed off. The wine was making itself known right away, and he had downed a couple of shots of bourbon before Maureen got home, only moments after the last remnants of the crime scene had been removed.

'Yesss?' she said picking up on what hadn't been spoken.

'Congratulations,' he said instead.

'Not at all adventurous, tonight?'

He shrugged.

'Chicken parmesan, right?'

'I've had enough adventure for the day.'

'We could have stayed home and I could have opened a can of SpaghettiOs.'

'I kind of like it this way. Candlelight, the scent of freshly baked bread, a hearty wine, a beautiful woman and a job.'

'A job? When?'

'Now. I don't know if it pays yet, but I have work.'

'What kind of work?'

'Murder.'

Maureen's face went blank. 'What?'

'Murder.'

'Where? When?'

'In our driveway. This afternoon.'

Four

Maureen couldn't sleep. She was full of questions. The answers, as much as Shanahan was able to provide, spawned wild speculation and still more questions. Shanahan was tired and inadequate.

'When are you going to talk to Jennifer Bailey?' Maureen didn't know her, but knew of her, heard the tales.

'I don't know. Her sister is just a few hours dead. What's the etiquette?'

Shanahan didn't have to fret about protocol. Bailey called him at seven a.m., dragging him out of bed. Shanahan left a languid, sleeping Maureen in her oblivion and picked up the phone. He tried to sound awake. He walked as she talked, pushing the button on the coffee maker as he did.

'Why did my sister want to talk to you?'

'I was hoping you could fill me in on that one.'

'You didn't speak at all?'

'She didn't quite make it to the door,' Shanahan said perhaps a little too coldly. He had wanted to give his condolences, but the time had already passed and her tone didn't invite sentiment or intimacy.

'I don't like talking on the phone.' They had that in common. 'Could you come out and see

16

me?' she asked with all the subtlety of a direct order.

'I don't drive anymore.'

'Oh,' she said, making the word sound like a thud.

'I'll find . . .'

'My car will pick you up nine. Is that OK?'

'I can do that.' He wanted to explain, but she had already disconnected.

Jennifer Bailey, a bony, slender body in a gray tailored suit, was built like her sister. How else they shared physical resemblance, he didn't know. After not finding a pulse, he purposefully didn't look at the victim's face. He had enough experience with dead bodies to know she was dead and enough experience with dead bodies not to add another face to the list.

'You don't have a car?' she asked as he slid in beside her in the back seat of a big Lexus.

'License. Brain surgery, possible seizures.'

'You plan to work?'

The driver, a heavy-set black man with silver hair and wearing a gray suit as well, did his best not to pay attention.

'I hadn't until your sister called.'

'You were going to take her case.'

'Probably not, but telling her "no" on the telephone turned out to be an option not on the table. In person, I thought she might be able to figure it out.'

Jennifer Bailey smiled. 'And as a favor to me? Thank you. Are you in pain?'

'No.'

17

'How's your thinking?'

'Others are going to have to evaluate that.'

'So far so good,' she said to Shanahan. And then, louder, 'Harold, up to the Butler area.'

'Would your sister tell you if she was in trouble?' Shanahan asked.

'I was surprised she wanted a recommendation for a PI.'

'She didn't tell you why?'

'She didn't, but that wasn't unexpected. We lived separate lives.'

'You two like each other?'

'You remain a smart aleck, but it is a good question, I'll give you that. We were competitive. That trumped a lot of things. We didn't share our innermost feelings.'

'But you talked?'

'Sure, there was family, her daughter, her daughter's children.'

'Did you argue?'

She smiled. 'I didn't kill her, Mr Shanahan. We rarely argued. I think we held a view of the world in common.'

'What was that?'

'That some folks just want to get by, be left alone. That some want more than they are entitled to and will do what they have to do to get it, whatever it is, and some are victims because they are too trusting, want to be liked, or just not too bright. She and I both wanted to level things a bit, though in different ways, she through good works and I through the law.'

It wasn't the first time she thought about that. There was a moment of quiet as the car angled

18

left from Emerson to Kessler Boulevard, where it angled north and west and where the neighborhood's average household income began to climb.

'Why me?' Shanahan asked.

'I think you're a bit like us,' she said. 'Only you have to be nudged a little bit. She asked me to find someone to help her. Someone she could trust. She emphasized trust over everything else.'

'Including competence.'

'Yes,' she said looking him squarely in the eyes. 'Did that hurt?'

'I'm not as fragile as I look. No other clue?'

'No.'

'You didn't ask?'

'She intimated that it would be best if I played no part in this. Whatever it was.'

'Or is.'

'Or is. I'm not sure how far I want to go with this, but, for now, I'd like for you to find out why she wanted to hire you. Just why. I want to be clear. I'm not hiring you to complete her investigation, just find out what that investigation was about.'

'I'm not sure I can. It's most likely a murder investigation.'

'Technically I'm not hiring you to find her murderer, but simply what was bothering her. A thin line, I know, but I can make it work, Mr Shanahan. I still have some connections. If you're game.' She gave Harold the address and the car headed into the Butler–Tarkington neighborhood.

'The police won't like our looking around the victim's home before they do.'

'They won't know.' She looked at her watch. 'We have an hour and a half before they arrive. I'm scheduled to meet them on the front porch at eleven.'

The city's north side up from 38th Street was thick with green lawns and multicolored leaves, some of them twittering to earth as the Lexus drove by. The homes, many of them decent-sized brick structures, were built in what Maureen called the Tudor style.

'I don't remember when it was the Tudors invaded Indianapolis, but they left their mark,' she told him once. Realty humor. It was true. These sturdy-looking, pointy brick and stone homes were everywhere and came in all sizes. Miniature towers, slate roofs. However, on the quiet street where Alexandra Fournier lived, there was greater variety of styles and they ranged from modest, single-level frame homes to not-quite mansions. Fournier's home fell into the latter category and it wasn't Tudor, but a handsome, unfussy, red-brick, two-story colonial. In front were a mature holly tree and a sapling of some sort. Sculpted evergreens stood on either side of the small porch.

Harold pulled into the drive.

'You know,' Shanahan said to his seat mate, 'you were the only one who knew she was coming to see me.'

'I didn't know when.' She smiled as if she had successfully volleyed a difficult shot.

'Who else would know?'

She didn't answer right away. Harold opened

20

the car door for her. She went to the front door. Shanahan followed.

'Sounds like a good place to start an investigation,' she said as she rummaged through her purse, finally pulling out a ring with dozens of keys. 'You can have Harold and the car from noon to eight for the next few days.' She found a key and inserted it into the lock. 'I'll pay the going rate.'

The door opened. A gush of fresh, cool air greeted them.

Five

Bailey led the way. The carpeted stairway began in the center of the entry hall. To the right was a wide opening and inside was a formal dining room. An opening to the left revealed what appeared to be a living room. Pale rose and smoky blues dominated the color scheme. A thick, soft, loosely upholstered sofa and two similarly covered chairs meant that, at home, comfort won out over clean lines.

Narrower halls on either side of the stairs led to the back of the house. Logic suggested a kitchen behind the dining room. And a parlor or den behind the living room into which Bailey disappeared. He caught her movement as she again went out of view behind a Japanese screen. He followed.

A book, *A Beautiful Mystery* by Louise Penny, was open, pages face down on the sofa pillow. An afghan was tossed carelessly over an arm of the sofa. A pot of mums occupied a side table beneath a window. Shanahan noted one could easily peer in. There were no signs she had taken any extra safety precautions.

'What a mess,' he heard her say.

Why didn't he kill her here? he asked himself, heading in the direction of Bailey's voice. 'What?' he said, approaching her.

'Nothing,' Bailey said, looking around. She seemed lost or confused.

22

Shanahan stepped into what was obviously Mrs Fournier's home office. Filing cabinet drawers were open as were desk drawers. Items on the desk were askew, but not wildly so. It was an organized search.

'She wouldn't have left things this way,' Bailey said.

The disarray, such as it was, was limited to the center of the room. The shelves that lined two of the walls were undisturbed. That's when he noticed the muddy hand print on the glass window that occupied most of the back wall. There was a clear image of a hand, the palm midway up the window, and it was clear that the hand had slipped down, leaving a smudged trail.

Shanahan approached the window warily. He was pretty sure what he would find. He wanted desperately to be wrong.

The boy was maybe sixteen. His cheekbone lay against the brick, but his head was cocked back. His eyes were frozen wide open, staring up to the cold, gray sky in surprise or possibly in horror. The kid was dead. A very thin red line, from what Shanahan could see, appeared as a ring around his neck. A wire, or garrote, had been used. He'd seen this sort of thing before.

'Miss Bailey, could you go out front and ask Harold to call Lieutenant Swann and tell him to get out here right away.'

Bailey moved toward him and the window. She looked. She shut her eyes, looked away. She took a deep breath.

'I'll do it,' Shanahan said. 'Come with me.' She didn't move. 'Come with me,' he said firmly and took her skinny arm. She began to cry. Her body shook.

'It's too much,' she said.

'It is,' he said. He held her for a moment; this brittle woman was now mush.

'Shanahan!'

The detective heard it, turned to see Swann approach. He and Bailey were on the front porch. Shanahan was glad for another, living face to replace the boy's. He stepped down to greet Swann. Harold watched, but stayed in the car.

'You go inside?' Swann asked.

Jennifer Bailey came up to them.

'I wanted to make sure I had the right key,' she said. 'I went in.'

'And you went around back?' Swan asked Shanahan. His tone hadn't changed.

'Stretch my legs,' Shanahan said.

'Something is being stretched,' Swann said. 'You're not investigating?'

'I've hired him to help me clean up my sister's affairs,' Bailey said curtly.

'If you don't mind my saying so, that's an attorney's or accountant's job.'

'I'm an attorney, Lieutenant. Given the circumstances, I need to tie up some loose ends.'

'What might those be?'

'Private. Family matters. I'm sure you understand.' It was an order, not a statement of fact.

Shanahan noticed she had relocated her steely core.

Swann nodded politely.

*　　*　　*

24

The second victim was identified as Nicky Hernandez, 17. Swann volunteered the name and address from the boy's wallet. On the way to Irvington to drop off a weary Jennifer Baily, she told Shanahan the young man was likely someone from one of the charities. Mrs Fournier would do that. She paid them to mow and trim and paint.

'Did she have offices elsewhere?'

'Where? What do you mean?' she asked, but her concentration was slipping away.

'Sometimes when you're involved with an organization, they might set aside a little corner of the office to . . . I don't know. What I'm trying to do is see who she met with before she was to meet me. Perhaps she stirred something up.'

'She could do that.'

Shanahan figured there was little to do with what was left of the afternoon. He asked Jennifer Bailey if she could call the organizations her sister worked with to vouch for Shanahan before he stopped by to ask questions. He gave her a copy of the faxes. The Civilian Crime Oversight Committee, designed to counter police abuse of power, was no doubt sensitive to the kinds of questions Shanahan would ask. Certainly a former attorney general would have some credibility. The nonprofits that involved the young might also be sensitive. Nobody trusted private detectives, including other private eyes. She could make access easier.

Then there was Judge Halston Fournier, deceased husband of victim number one. He

25

wanted some background on the man, but wanted it as objective as possible. He knew a lawyer. If James Fenimore Kowalski didn't have the skinny on the judge, he would know how to get it.

Shanahan had a plan – a rough one. Check out all of the victim's connections and try to figure out who she talked to right before her demise. He would work the police, though he didn't expect much. What the police would get from the murder scenes and the autopsies Shanahan believed would be little if any more than he had already. It was a professional job. No amateur could shoot that accurately from that distance. No amateur would have had, thought about, or even known how to use a garrote. It was the perfect weapon to silently kill someone in a residential neighborhood. This wasn't the work of someone operating on impulse. This was bad news. Shanahan had the skill to identify suspects and then narrow the list. But was he up to this kind of investigation?

Probably. His approach was motive driven, not based on sophisticated forensics. This might work here. And his range was local. He'd soon find out if he was out of his league. But the only motive a professional killer has is money. It would be the hitman's employer who would have a traceable motive. The man who pulled the trigger and cut the throat was long gone, a man who had no real connection to the victims and possibly no connection to whoever hired him.

Jennifer Baily had been wrung of any energy she might have had left after the gruesome morning. Any more time with her wouldn't be productive for either of them. Shanahan had Harold drop him off and pick up the faxes before the Lexus headed for the increasingly gentrified eastside neighborhood of Irvington and a nap for Mrs Jennifer Bailey.

It was still early in the day, but Shanahan felt no guilt pouring himself two fingers of J.W. Dant bourbon. He had handled the first murder well, the second not so well at all. Mrs Fournier had no idea what hit her. The young man had some time to feel the pain and contemplate his fate.

Six

Kowalski returned Shanahan's call in person. There was warning: the low, loud growl of the lawyer's Harley in the drive not only alerted a dozing Shanahan but neighbors far and wide as well.

Kowalski, always dressed in a shabby black suit and a white shirt; all he needed at any time was a tie and he was ready for court. He was a big man. His hair and beard were striped with silver. His presence, as if it were filled with compressed explosives, was intimidating. With him was a bottle of Powers Irish whiskey.

'None of your Kentucky sludge,' he said, helping himself to glasses from the kitchen. 'I hear you had your head sewn on?'

'Stapled,' Shanahan said, looking out of the window. Kowalski's black Harley was parked where Mrs Fournier went down.

'Stapled?'

'Twice.'

'Maybe you should consider Velcro.' He handed Shanahan a glass, took one with him to one of the upholstered chairs. 'You're still standing.'

There was a slow exquisite burn in Shanahan's throat.

'Sorry about Casey,' Kowalski said, rising his glass in a subtle toast. 'He's in heaven herding hogs. Catahoula, right?'

Shanahan nodded.

'Louisiana Leopard dog,' Kowalski added.

Shanahan nodded again.

'You think he ever saw Mardi Gras?'

'Probably not. He was pretty young when he showed up wanting board and room.'

'Not many of those around. Not many of you either, so stick around.'

'What do you know of Judge Halston Fournier?'

'You're on that? The murder of the judge's wife?'

Shanahan nodded.

'What's your take?'

'Professional.'

'Why?'

Shanahan shrugged.

'Tell me what you know and I'll tell you about her late husband.'

'Think that's a fair trade?' Shanahan asked. It was fine with Shanahan. It was a good idea to run his theories by a smart and crafty criminal defense attorney.

'And I'll leave the bottle when I go.'

'Deal.'

'The shooter is based not too far from here,' he said after hearing Shanahan's explanation. 'He most likely didn't fly in. Security is too tight. Not just the weapons problem, but way too many cameras. Like I said, he doesn't live too far from here, but most likely he doesn't live here either. Most hitmen don't kill where they live. So that means the hitter probably drove. No more than five hours away. Chicago. Detroit. Or some shack or house trailer in the middle of rural Podunk County in the land of the lost.'

That pretty much validated Shanahan's decision not to pursue the shooter and connect him to the person who hired him. Only the police could do that and probably only then if they worked with police departments in other cities. He'd talk with Collins.

'A garrote?' Kowalski asked himself in a near whisper. 'He knew when to use what tool, didn't he?'

'And the cold-hearted decision to use it.'

'Special training. You don't get that off video games. I don't think so, anyway.' Kowalski poured a little more whiskey in each of their glasses. 'The judge has been dead a couple of years.'

'I'm checking all the bases. What kind of enemies does a woman have when she has devoted her life to helping others? If her sister had been killed we'd look at the people she prosecuted.'

'We still should. And the judge's.' He sat back. 'Did you know that Halston – "Hall," as he was called – was Bailey's beau before he married Alexandra?'

Kowalski stayed on for dinner. He told bawdy, exaggerated tales of his most recent adventures.

'I didn't come up to see you in the hospital,' he said, downing the remnants of a hearty Cabernet. 'I don't do hospitals, unless it's visiting a client or witness. I don't do funerals. So, if you croak and are hovering round to see who shows up, don't expect to see me.'

'About the case,' Maureen said, emptying the bottle in Kowalski's glass. 'It wasn't the shooter's only job. He had to find something, right? That's why the kid was killed.'

'If there was something to be found, he found it,' Shanahan said.

'What makes you think so?' Kowalski asked.

'He started at her desk, judging by the level of disorder and worked his way out, but the files and shelves against the outer walls seemed to be undisturbed.'

'Unless,' Maureen said, 'he stopped when he realized the kid knew he was there.'

'Maybe. But he is cool as a cucumber . . .'

'You're going to have to update your clichés, Shanahan,' Kowalski said.

'He's a pro. If it was important enough to take the risk in the first place and then kill a witness to the search, it would be really frustrating not to get what you came for or at least finish searching for it.'

Kowalski left shortly before midnight. The man would wear him out, Shanahan thought, but given his druthers Shanahan was happier to have the man along for the ride.

Harold was there at noon.

'Your driver is here, Mr Shanahan,' Maureen said in a mock-snooty tone.

She was in good spirits. Last night had been good for her, for them. A little life and a little laughter in the silent, empty house.

Shanahan's attempt to climb into the front passenger seat was aborted when Shanahan saw that Harold used it for his laptop, a pair of sunglasses and a brown bag. Maybe lunch. Harold made no move to rearrange things. Shanahan sat, uncomfortably, in the back.

Not only was he in a luxury car, he was being driven around . . . and driven around by a black man in what could easily be regarded as a uniform. This kind of class-distinctive ostentation was not only bad for a business that usually prized anonymity if not outright invisibility, but it was a personal misstatement of Shanahan himself. He was not an 'upstairs, downstairs' kind of guy.

'Where to?' Harold asked.

Shanahan leaned forward, gave him the address of Daniel Holcomb, who aside from having his own private practice, was a senior member of the Public Safety and Criminal Justice Committee for the city, a group of folks ostensibly charged as a civilian police oversight committee, but without the teeth of being truly public or truly civilian. Holcomb was also on the City Council.

'Sit back and relax, Mr Shanahan. Enjoy and let me do the driving. It's what I do.'

It was a toss-up. They could go to Washington Street for a straight shot to downtown or, as Harold chose, cruise one-way Michigan Street downtown. The lights were timed so that if you went at thirty-five miles per hour you never saw a red light. Smooth as silk, Shanahan thought. Cool as a cucumber, he remembered.

Sitting back, Shanahan noticed a roll of fat at the base of Harold's neck and the broadness of his shoulders. Big and soft. His age was difficult to tell. But he was up there.

'Football?' Shanahan asked.

'Basketball,' Harold said. 'Crispus Attucks.'

'Oh? You know Oscar Robertson?'

'Met him. He was a couple of years ahead of me.'

'A couple?'

'Yeah, three years.'

Doing the math, Shanahan figured he and Harold were about the same age.

'You play college ball?'

'No. To go any farther I had to be either taller or faster, preferably both.' He laughed. 'I did go to college, but I had to pay for it.'

'This is your retirement, 'Shanahan said. 'Second career.'

'Right. Trooper. Thirty-five years with the state police.'

'That's how you came to drive for the attorney general.'

'You ask a lot of questions.'

'That's what I do. You ever drive for Miss Bailey's sister?'

'Never,' he said sharply. 'You done?'

'One more. Are you carrying?'

'It's legal. Problem?'

'Not for me.' He made a mental note to check Harold's background. He could ask Jennifer Bailey, but Shanahan didn't take anyone's 'word for it.' Not even his client's.

Seven

Daniel Holcomb could pass for under thirty, except for his eyes. They seemed much older. Shanahan wasn't sure whether they expressed wisdom or distrust. Perhaps both. Or maybe they were the same thing. Holcomb's hair was too long – slightly over the ears and in the back an inch or so beyond the shirt collar – to be an Indiana Republican.

He extended his hand. A firm but not crushing handshake, after which Shanahan was ushered to a sofa, away from Holcomb's desk, in the spacious office. The art on the walls looked expensive. Holcomb. Shanahan rummaged through his mind. He hadn't recognized the name or the photos that came with the stack of papers Maureen had created before breakfast. Then again, he didn't follow local politics. But now, Shanahan saw him as familiar. He was on TV periodically, the local news, and in the newspaper occasionally in a highlighted editorial. There was no doubt he was being groomed or had ambition for political office.

'You're a private investigator, right? How do you know Jennifer?' Holcomb asked in a friendly manner when they settled in.

'I did some work for her in the past.'

'For the state?'

'No,' Shanahan said, feeling the need to be on

the other side of the interrogation. 'I'm looking into the death of her sister. She said you would help. Will you?'

That did it.

'Of course.'

If Holcomb sought a career in politics as a Democrat, he would need Jennifer Bailey's support. She was not only highly respected by the base and could rally the black vote, as a former attorney general she had to be privy to a lot of information that could either help or damage a rising star.

'Was Alexandra Fournier, who was on your civilian oversight committee, particularly interested in a specific case or cases?' Shanahan asked.

'You think her death might be connected to our investigations?' He picked up a carafe of water and with ceremonial formality poured two glasses. It was clear Holcomb wanted control of the conversation. Shanahan knew the technique from his intelligence days. Holcomb was a lawyer, wasn't he? Shanahan thought. Basic instinct.

'I have no idea. However, among all her associations, all her board and charity work, her work with you—'

'With the committee,' he said, interrupting.

'—has the greatest capacity to generate highly passionate opinions in cases where police, prone to violence, are the prime players.'

'Provided there were problems.' He sat back.

'It's a political minefield.'

'Can be, I suppose. I don't recall any significant disagreements.'

'Maybe there are others on the committee who have a different perspective.'

He leaned forward again. 'I'm not sure what you're saying.'

'Unless it's a rubber-stamp committee, there would have to be divisive cases. Because there are cops involved and their careers and pensions are on the line and because there are both bleeding-heart liberals and law-and-order-at-any-cost conservatives on your committee, there would have to be disagreements about the disposition of cases, Mr Holcomb. So I'll ask you again. Are you going to help us?'

'Us?'

'My client. Miss Bailey, and me.'

Holcomb looked at his watch. If Shanahan had that watch, he'd hock it and buy Maureen a new car.

'Have you had lunch?' Holcomb asked.

'I've got a crowded afternoon.' Shanahan lied to counter the lawyer's attempt at misdirection. He no doubt wanted time to think about what he should and should not say.

'I can have it sent up.'

'No, thanks.'

'You mind if I go ahead?'

He went to his desk, picked up the phone. 'Chicken salad on rye. Yogurt.' He headed back to the sofa. 'Now, let's start over.'

Starting over was OK with Shanahan. More time. Less tension. Considering the expensive office and attire, Shanahan was using up a very expensive attorney's time, probably billed in excess of

36

a thousand an hour. That's why he was squeezing it in over lunch. It didn't matter to Shanahan. The old detective relented.

'I didn't realize there was so much profit in criminal law,' Shanahan said, making a broad gesture to the office.

'There are rich criminals,' Holcomb said, smiling.

'But they so rarely get caught.'

'We tend to take on white-collar crime cases here. It's a specialty. A different approach than an assault or drug charge. And we do other things as well.'

'So tell me if there are some explosive cases that should be looked into.'

Holcomb's take – 'and you didn't get this from me,' he said, promising to deny it if need be – was that there was only one case generating the kind of high heat that could lead to homicide. Officer Leonard Card, a member of IMPD's Criminal Gang Unit, and twenty years on the job, killed a young black kid, who according to subsequent investigation had no gang connections. Card had a history of abuse charges and had been involved in other deaths, for which he had been cleared. Then again, as Shanahan knew, most of these cases are just for show. Police, even more than most closed societies – doctors, firefighters and judges, for example – protect their own.

Shanahan would run this by a couple of other randomly chosen members on the committee to see if Holcomb left out anything or anyone important.

Next stop, Second Chance Community. According to Bailey, while police oversight was her duty – an unpleasant but necessary task – her sister was devoted to SCC. She founded the organization. It was her and her late husband's legacy.

Eight

Descending from the gilt-edged environs of Daniel Holcomb in the heart of the increasingly high-rise downtown to the flea-market décor of Second Chance Community could cause the bends in a more sensitive man. Shanahan had no trouble with the transition. The manager of SCC, Margaret Tice, was twice the size of Mr Holcomb. Other than her sturdiness, she was unremarkable. Her face was without age lines. Her eyes were small and did not peer into Shanahan's soul or allow a glimpse into her own. Her lips never found a smile or any other emotion. She was, on the other hand, matter-of-factly open and helpful.

She showed Shanahan around.

'There are several old houses on what we call the campus. We have recreation areas, a place to play basketball, a softball diamond, some class rooms, though our boys and girls attend public school if at all possible.'

Shanahan followed her outside. Across the street were dilapidated houses, some boarded up. And down on the corner was a cluster of shops, probably once a small grocery and maybe a dry cleaners and hardware. All were closed except for the liquor store.

'Some of the kids live here?' Shanahan asked.

'Oh yes. Most are unadoptable and have run through the foster care programs.'

'Troublemakers?' Shanahan asked.

'The troubled ones.' She had corrected him, but her tone suppressed any hint of admonition. 'We keep them busy. The houses across the street are going to be torn down. Mrs Fournier bought the land, was going to lease it to us for a dollar a year. We're turning it into a community garden. Probably more like a farm. Corn, tomatoes, all sorts of produce.'

'In the middle of the city,' Shanahan said.

'Yes,' she said. 'Turning things around.'

'Where is everyone?' he asked.

'School.'

Shanahan looked at his watch. 'So you have a couple of hours of quiet this time of day.'

'Always things to do.'

'Can you tell me about Nicky Hernandez?' He followed her.

They entered one of the indoor recreation areas, an old living room/parlor with a ping-pong table, a couple of beat-up sofas, card tables, a big screen TV in each room. Two old computers perched on another table.

'You know,' she said, sitting on the arm of a sofa, 'when your family treats you like crap from the day you're born and all the people outside treat you like crap – clerks, cops, teachers – it's damn hard not to turn out as anything but crap.'

'Nicky?'

'He was at the door to a new life. The door was open. And he almost made it.' She shook her head. 'He had that spark. He could've made it.'

'Mrs Fournier?'

40

'She believed in him. She believed in all of them. But Nicky turned seventeen. He didn't have much time left here. They have to go at eighteen. She hired him to do odd jobs. Build some savings, start references for a resume.'

'Was that the first time he did yard work for her?'

'No. He did her yard from spring to winter for some years. In the winter he shoveled snow. Rain or shine he'd be there once a week. Wednesdays. Every Wednesday. Early in the morning. She . . . Mrs Fournier was a creature of habit.'

'How did he get there?'

'She'd pick him up. She'd come by early. Real early.'

'It must be tough losing them both.'

'It makes no sense.'

'Without Mrs Fournier, how will this all keep going?'

'It's set up to do what we do. It's solid. Endowments. Trusts. But without her we won't have her guidance, her influence in the community.'

'You have no idea why anyone would want to kill her?'

'No. Or him,' she said. 'Good people. No harm to anyone them being alive. I simply don't understand.'

'Could I see his room?'

'His bed,' she said. 'No one has rooms except the staff.'

Shanahan was surprised. He was running out of breath. His steps were shorter. She had to slow down a not particularly fast gait so he could catch

41

up. He hadn't done anything strenuous. But now, as he thought about it, this was his first day out.

The steps to the second floor were hard and he had to stop to catch his breath on the landing, where the stairway turned.

'You OK?'

'Just time catching up with me.'

'The police were here,' she said. 'Didn't stay long.'

There was a bed with a wool blanket and a trunk. Just like basic training, he remembered. There was a padlock on what the Army called a 'footlocker.'

'You mind?' He knelt down and pulled a small leather case from his pocket and from that a slender metal tool. She didn't object. A couple of pairs of jeans. T-shirts. Sweatshirts. A clean pair of athletic shoes. Some toiletries in a plastic bag. A picture calendar – one of the freebies from a travel agency. Sunsets, palm trees and a page to write in appointments. Shanahan thumbed through it as best he could with his half-numb left hand and its nearly useless fingers. 'Mrs Fournier' was penciled in several of the little boxes, every Wednesday throughout the year, including the day Nicky Hernandez was killed.

'Police didn't take anything?' Shanahan asked, using the footlocker to help himself stand. Even then his arms shook. Muscles in his arms and legs refused to live up to his expectations. He faltered and nearly fell. She caught him, held onto his arms, until he felt balance and strength return. What an embarrassment.

'They didn't really seem interested,' she said,

still appraising his condition. 'I think they write off these kids. The ones that end up here just don't seem to be worth the effort.'

Shanahan found his balance – enough of it, at least, to stand without help.

'You're old enough to remember those *Saturday Evening Post* magazine covers where the policeman is giving a lost young boy an ice-cream cone.'

Margaret walked him to the car. 'It was a fairy tale, even then,' she said, 'certainly in the poor, black neighborhoods.'

Harold, perhaps sensing something was wrong, got out and opened the back door. Margaret looked puzzled. The Lexus wasn't quite a limo, but looked pretty upscale for the neighborhood. And Shanahan didn't look like he was to the manor born.

'I think we'll end a little early today,' Shanahan said to Harold. He was running on empty.

Nine

Shanahan opened his eyes. Daylight was gone. There was a sharp-edged triangle of light on the hardwood floor. It was all disorienting for a moment.

'Want a whiskey?' Maureen asked, kindly but uncharacteristically. Her shadow took up part of the triangle.

'How long have you been here?'

'A couple of hours. I came in. You were sitting there, straight up, head bowed. I checked to see if you were dead.'

'Was I?'

'Yes. This is heaven. Funny though, I thought heaven would be snazzier. Whiskey?'

'Thanks. No.'

'Must've been a bad day.'

'Just more of it than I counted on.'

She headed back toward the kitchen.

'Wait, Maureen.' She turned. 'You thought heaven would be *snazzy*?'

'Snazzy. Yes. You?' she asked.

'I thought there'd be a swimming pool, at least.'

He debated calling Jennifer Bailey and begging off the case. Instead he found himself asking her who was Holcomb's opposite number on the oversight committee.

'Regina Thompkins,' Bailey said without hesitation. 'She's going to run for mayor.'

44

'And so is Holcomb,' Shanahan said.

'Yes.'

'And the winner is . . .'

'Too early to tell if they'll get the nominations. But she's willing to go all the way to the right to get one. There's always a chance she'll go too far. And because Holcomb can be all things to all people, she'd like it to be anyone but him. You think this is political? The deaths?'

'Just need to know what motivates people. There's potential for a connection on your sister's police oversight committee.'

'Let me know. And don't mention my name to Mrs Thompkins. We're not on friendly terms.'

Shanahan followed up with phone calls to Mrs Thompkins. Couldn't get in. She wasn't in. She would get back to him. She was in a meeting. She would get back to him. On a conference call. She would get back to him.

He got in touch with Kowalski, who agreed that for a minor fee he would have his assistant run down some information. On Leonard Card, the cop, Daniel Holcomb, the defense attorney, Mrs Thompkins, the busy real estate agent and housewife, Judge Fournier, Jennifer Baily and perhaps her driver and bodyguard, Harold.

Just before noon, Shanahan thought Mrs Thompkins was due for an ambush. Maureen plucked her photo from the city government's web page. She was the perfect embodiment of a professional Republican woman. A red, tailored jacket, harshly drawn eyebrows, very red lips and very disciplined blonde hair that might have been a helmet.

She wouldn't be easy.

'Scary,' he said.

'What's scary?'

'Her. Her hair. It's too scared to move.'

Maureen laughed. 'Listen, she's in real estate. I've picked a couple of expensive homes. She's the listing agent. That means she gets a bundle of money if she sells it herself. So pick a property she listed and ask her about it, push to see her. Then, do your magic.'

'Magic?'

'How do you feel?' she asked.

'Fine, but not necessarily magical.' He felt a little light-headed, but this was common after taking his morning pills. The feeling would last maybe thirty minutes.

Before Harold picked him up at noon, Shanahan received a call from a young woman, Kowalski's assistant, with some information: the address of the cop under investigation; his background, which included a number of abuse complaints and his scores on various tests, including those from the firing range. Shanahan drew the profile of a lazy cop lifer who was a natural bully, not exceedingly bright and who couldn't have pulled off the murder of Alexandra Fournier. The messenger passed along a request that Shanahan stop by Kowalski's place before calling it a day.

Harold took a sip of his coffee before backing down the drive. Neither driver nor passenger was the talkative type, and Shanahan figured he had gotten all he could from him. He hoped Harold's few missing years would be less mysterious after the afternoon meeting with Kowalski.

'Where to?'

Shanahan told him.

Leonard Card lived on Lincoln Road in an area known as Wynnedale. The house was a ranch-style home, wood frame on three sides with a strange brick and limestone face behind over-grown shrubbery. Drapery over the picture window had been pulled closed. A slightly banged up, gray Jeep Cherokee was in the drive. Behind it was a dirty, silver or gray, late-model Malibu.

Harold parked in front, busied himself with his computer as Shanahan made his way to the front door.

Leonard Card looked nothing like Shanahan thought he would. From his record, Shanahan pictured a dark, hairy thickset guy with blood-shot eyes. What he saw was a tall, thin, fit man with a shaved head, piercing blue eyes and a substantial, hooked nose. He looked like a bird of prey. Instead of a taciturn dullness, he appeared sharp, aware. Dangerous.

'Yeah?' He looked out over Shanahan's shoulder, no doubt picking up on Harold.

That was probably good.

'Dietrich Shanahan, private investigator.'

'I don't want any,' he said, stepping back, ready to shut the door.

'How do you know?'

The answer was a silent sullen stare. A cop's default expression, the look didn't mean much.

'You going to make it through the hearing?' Shanahan asked. 'I understand the kid you killed wasn't a gang member.'

Card's eyes went back out to the Lexus. 'Who's he?' Card asked.

'My keeper,' Shanahan said. 'I'm looking into things. Maybe I'll turn up something that will help. Maybe I'll turn up something that won't.'

'Who do you work for?'

'Someone who wants to see things turn out right. That kind of thing help you?'

'Right is in the eye of the beholder.'

'You wanna talk?' Shanahan asked.

Card didn't blink. He just shut the door.

'You have trouble making friends,' Harold said, handing Shanahan a slip of paper. The detective shut the car door as his chauffeur started the engine.

The name 'Samantha Byers' was written out as well as an address in South Bend, Indiana. In fact it was on US Highway 31.

'The silver Malibu,' Harold said, shutting the lid to his laptop. 'Where to?'

'Keystone and eighty-sixth.'

Lots of trees in the neighborhood, Shanahan thought. The quick and brutal cold wave of a few weeks ago had taken its toll. Some of the older trees, especially the ones that bore fruit, weren't going to make it. Death lingered under bright, rich colors.

'Anything else on Samantha?'

'Absolutely zero. Good girl, it seems.'

'Can't be too good if she's with Card.'

Mrs Thompkins's office, as nice as it was, seemed downmarket compared to Daniel

48

Holcomb's. She was obviously fond of straight lines and bold colors.

'What brought you to us, Mr Shanahan?' she asked as she escorted him to a glass-topped table. Two chairs faced a large-screen computer. He sat in one. She remained standing.

'The house in William's Creek I mentioned to your assistant,' Shanahan said.

'Can I get you something to drink?'

'No, thank you,' Shanahan said. 'I like to focus on the business at hand. How firm is the price?'

She sat beside him, clicked some keys until the $3.2 million home popped up.

'It's only been on the market for a couple of weeks. But I take any offer seriously.' She clicked and a slide show began. 'You're not working with a realtor? Seriously?'

'Seriously.'

'I assume,' she said, allowing a small – perhaps flirtatious – smile to escape, 'you would like to see it before you buy it.'

'I heard you were running for mayor.'

She clicked off the computer, looked down at the tabletop momentarily. 'You're wasting my time.'

'I'm registered to vote.'

'Maybe I should call the police.'

'Who said I'm not interested in the house?'

'Could you possibly afford it?'

'I could get a second job,' Shanahan said.

'And you're first is?'

'Investigator. Looking into deaths linked to the Civilian Review Board.'

'Deaths?'

'Alexandra Fournier,' Shanahan said.

'Oh my God. You think there is a connection?' She looked surprised, upset, nervous.

'That's what I'm trying to figure out. How well did you know Mrs Fournier?'

'Not well. I understood where she was coming from, but we agreed on very little. I'm sure that doesn't surprise you. Listen, Mr Dietrich . . .'

'Shanahan, Dietrich Shanahan . . .'

'I'll let you know if I find out anything that might help. Give me your card, if you would. Also' – she extended her hand – 'I'll be taking your calls from now on.'

He didn't want to like her and he knew the first thing a politician learns is to fake sincerity, yet he believed that what he told her did shock her and that she wasn't brushing him off.

'Mrs Fournier was very interested in the idea of young people getting second chances to straighten out their lives. She might have taken a special interest in the case of Officer Leonard Card.'

'Card?' She appeared to be searching her memory.

'Leonard Card's case is about the shooting of a young innocent bystander . . .'

'Oh, yes. We have more than one case. We don't know "innocent" or not, hence the investigation,' she said.

'Any witnesses? A partner?' Shanahan asked, searching for another way into the case against Card.

'He was undercover. And you? I've been forthcoming. Who are you working for?'

'Can't tell you.'

'Holcomb?'

'You earned that at least. No. Not Holcomb, but it is interesting that you bring him up.'

The walk across the parking lot provided fair warning. Shanahan's energy was already waning. He hadn't exerted himself. Slow walking. A little talking. Was it his brain or maybe the medication? He wasn't in pain. He was simply drained of the life force, he thought. Life force.

He and Harold stopped at a Burger King, something he could not do with Maureen. Though it wasn't a huge sacrifice he made for the woman he loved, he occasionally craved the big fish sandwich with cheese. And just as she secretly devoured pistachio ice cream, he would do the same with a fat fish sandwich from a fast-food chain. This time and for the first time he could only get through half of it.

It occurred to Shanahan as he walked the evidence of their guilty pleasure to the trash that he had allowed his investigation to center around Leonard Card. It certainly was a connection, but Alexandra Fournier lived a fuller life. She had strong political opinions, owned property. Could there be an inheritance issue?

Perhaps Kowalski would have something.

They weren't moving. Shanahan opened his eyes. He could see the back of Harold's head. Wires led to his ears and tiny earphones. It was deadly quiet. Outside was a river carrying a

51

couple of dead tree limbs southward. It took
him a moment, but Shanahan realized he'd
dozed off again. He was at Kowalski's place
without witnessing the trip. He could get used
to that kind of travel.

Ten

'I was worried you went and died on me,' Harold said.

Shanahan saw Harold's eyes in the rearview mirror.

'I get that a lot. How long was I out?'

'An hour maybe. We're just a few blocks from the address you gave me.'

'Good. We'll pay Mr Kowalski a visit and call it a day.'

'Miss Bailey called. She wants to see you before you go home.'

Kowalski shared his riverfront home with a bulldog who seemed to have the same regard for consciousness as Shanahan. Kowalski, in Shanahan's eyes, was a bulldog too, looking a little more ferocious than he was, but extremely formidable if provoked.

Kowalski greeted him with two glasses of Irish whiskey, keeping one for himself.

'Life is good,' Kowalski said, stepping to one side. 'It is important we keep it that way.'

Shanahan didn't know what music was playing softly in the background, but it was pleasant. So was the art on the walls. He'd have to be careful not to drift off again, he reminded himself as he sank deeply onto the worn cushions of the leather sofa.

'So, let's get to it,' Kowalski said, glancing down at a yellow legal pad. 'The do-gooder sister, Alexandra, had a ton of money, or assets actually. Judge Fournier bought up property all over town, mostly low-rent, abandoned. He wasn't a slum-lord and there's no indication that he bought these with any insider knowledge about the future. But some of it has proven profitable and more of it might as city populations are becoming more urban centered.

'Your client, Jennifer Bailey, though you wouldn't know by looking, is the poor sister. Not only did she lose the judge, she missed out on his investments. Miss Bailey is not going to starve, but she might have to give up hiring private eyes and personal drivers unless the will favors her with a generous bequest.'

Kowalski raised his eyebrows to emphasize the possible murder motive contained in his words. He flipped the page and continued. 'There is a brother out there somewhere.' He shook his head, shrugged. 'Maybe he'll bubble up to the surface when they read the will.

'Both Thompkins and Holcomb are who they say they are,' Kowalski said. 'For the most part. Thompkins probably doesn't care who sleeps with whom, but claims to be against same-sex marriage when pressed. She's a friend to the rich in their times of need. Chamber of Commerce princess. Holcomb is what we used to call a limousine liberal. Not sure how comfortable he is with the great unwashed masses, but he talks a good game. Trust fund baby. Art collector, donor to the arts. The

Kennedy school of charm and not subject to the sins of the fathers. Father made it big in commercial real estate, especially in Chicago and the region. Holcomb is a criminal defense attorney, but his are higher-end criminals and most of his skill is making sure there is no time served and reducing fines. Dealing with the guys I deal with would probably scare him to death. Both are on the City Council.'

Kowalski refilled the glasses, then arranged some logs in the fire, which seemed to energize the dog, who waddled over to inspect.

'He loves this time of day,' Kowalski said. 'Cigar?'

'No, thanks.'

'No deep, dark secrets I could find,' Kowalski said. 'The cop, Card, is a creep. The usual. Loves the power. Loves to hurt people. But usually stays just this side of the line. I can't imagine him killing the kid on purpose. Not because it would cause him sleepless nights. Too much paperwork.'

Kowalski lit a match, touched it to the newspaper stuffed under the logs, at strategic spots. It took only seconds for the fire to take off.

'It's an art,' he said no doubt considering a bow to his audience during a hot, white burst of flame.

When the flames retreated to a steady burn, the dog moved in, dropped down on its belly, closed its eyes and opened its mouth, whereupon his mammoth tongue escaped its confinement.

Kowalski retrieved the legal pad; one more flip of the page.

'Finally, Harold B. Vincent. High school all-star. Scholarship to Purdue. His basketball star status faded in his junior year. He went into the military where he served with, as they say, distinction. He *was* Special Forces, Shanahan. The real thing. He got out, finished his college and went to work for the state police . . . no doubt where he met Miss Attorney General.'

'His record with the police?'

'Solid. Duty with the governor's office. Before that with missing children. Decent retirement. If his tastes aren't too extravagant, he's in good shape for his golden years.'

Irvington is an old neighborhood. Once abandoned during the era of urban flight, its handsome, well-constructed homes and mature trees invited gentrification. Jennifer Bailey occupied one of the grand old two-story homes. The home had a similar sense of propriety to that of her deceased sister's, though it wouldn't bring half the sale price.

Odd, Shanahan thought as he went toward the frail woman standing in the front doorway. Jennifer had a late model car and a driver, while Alexandra was content with an old Buick she drove herself.

The expression on Miss Bailey's face wasn't pleasant. She didn't invite him in. It seemed to him that she was, in fact, blocking the door.

'I have learned that you have been asking questions about me?'

'Yes,' Shanahan replied.

'Why?'

'Due diligence.'

'You don't trust me?'

'Trust isn't in my job description. Or yours.'

'I'm paying you to investigate me? And Harold?'

'The fact is, Miss Bailey, you might not know if someone hates you or resents you or wants something from you. Harold seems like a nice enough guy, but who knows? I like to know who I'm dealing with.'

'What did you find out?' she asked.

'That, apparently, you still have connections. I'll have to be more careful.'

'Mr Shanahan, have you been drinking?'

Shanahan thought about ignoring the question, but decided some lines had to be drawn.

'Some very fine Irish whiskey.'

'On my dime?'

'I do business my way. Sometimes having a drink with someone is the best way to get information or simply an enjoyable way to pass the time. If you wanted a teetotaler, maybe you should have hired a Mormon.'

'I forgot,' she said.

'What?'

'Time had erased the memory of some of your sharper edges.'

'All coming back to you now?'

'We'll proceed your way for the time being,' she said. 'Harold! Please take Mr Shanahan home.'

Shanahan headed for the Lexus. He stopped. 'Who is the beneficiary of your sister's estate?'

'We'll find out tomorrow.'

'Her daughter?'

'They had a falling out.'

'There are photos of young kids in her wallet. Birthday parties.'

'Probably from the center. She disowned the lot of them. She could be stubborn.'

'You didn't disown them.'

'No. I did not.'

Shanahan's house on Pleasant Run was what they used to call 'a stone's throw' from Irvington. He managed to stay awake during the short trip. He thought about Jennifer Bailey, a highly respected attorney who knew nothing about her sister's will. He thought about tomorrow, as unsure of its arrival as he'd ever been and he thought about Maureen, about how his increasing frailty could exacerbate the already existing issue of his age and hers; though the issue as far as he knew was in his mind only.

He napped, the whiskey softly coating his inflamed Irish brain.

'Good.' She nodded at the usual spaghetti carbonara he had learned to make. 'And how was the day?'

'Visited with Kowalski's bulldog.'

'And Kowalski?'

'Him too. As well as the lady, Tompkins.'

'What was she like?'

'She came around.'

'What does that mean?' Maureen seemed almost angry.

'She softened a bit. Her eyebrows looked like

58

they were tattooed on, her lipstick applied by a sign painter, the lines were so perfect.'

'And . . .?'

'That's intimidating.'

'She's tough.' Maureen grinned. 'That's her reputation.'

'You cross paths?' Shanahan asked.

'She serves a different clientele.'

'If I give you an address, can you get me a phone number?' he asked.

'Isn't that part of your bag of tricks?'

'Used to be. I'm an old dog and I don't understand the new tricks at all.'

Shanahan cleared the table. It was a slow process because his left hand still refused to follow commands. He had broken a half-dozen dishes so far.

Maureen retrieved her laptop and returned to sip her wine and begin her search. She squinted at the little piece of paper he had given her and her fingers danced over the keys, clinking.

'No Samantha Byers in South Bend,' she said. 'Who's she?'

'Somebody playing house or hanging out with a troubled cop.'

'The address belongs to Benzie's Motel.'

'Benzie's?'

'You know it?' Maureen asked.

'A divey place just outside South Bend's city limits. I'll be damned. You have a number?'

'And how do you know such a dive so easily when you can't even remember what you had for breakfast?'

'I have a divey past.'

'No one here by that name,' said the man who answered the phone at Benzie's.

'You remember her?'

'No time for nostalgia.' The man was gone. Samantha was off the grid. She checked into a motel just long enough to register her car so she had legit plates and registration if she's pulled over for speeding, but that's it. Maybe she moved in with Leonard Card.

'Maybe a prostitute,' Maureen said. 'An escort working Indianapolis and Chicago.'

Cops and working girls, Shanahan thought, a natural combination. They work the same streets, interact in the games of petty crimes. Acts of extremely personal violence and intimacy with strangers. Lonely night shifts. Pretend to be tough. Pretend to be turned on. So much in common.

'Maybe,' Shanahan said.

He was still awake when she came to bed. Except on the coldest nights, she slept nude. He watched as she casually revealed herself, the golden incandescence from the lamp on the bedside table warming her flesh and the room. He was so old, and aging so rapidly, while she was no older than she was when they met. Was he being fair?

No. Not in the least. Not only about her living a fuller, more vibrant life, but about Shanahan likely putting her in danger. He had poked the beehive. It was likely that was what Mrs Fournier had done. Look what happened to her.

The light went out in the bedroom. He felt her slide against him, her lips touched his ear.

'I'm with you for life. Yours. Mine. The earth's.'

Eleven

Shanahan awoke determined. As Maureen enjoyed the gray morning under the covers, he called Jennifer Bailey, telling her to drop by and pick him up for the reading of the will.

'That won't be necessary,' she said curtly. 'I'll let you know what happens.'

'I need to be there,' Shanahan said.

'Why is that?'

'There are things you might not see.'

'I don't think . . .'

'What time will you be by?'

Jennifer Bailey was an attractive, elegant, even noble woman. She was also used to getting her way. She wouldn't waste a moment on false civility. The ride downtown was silent.

The law offices were located on the fourteenth floor of a handsome neo-gothic building with a gaudy ground-floor bank – Hunter's Bank – stealing its architectural purity and respectability. Their blue-and-orange signs were appearing everywhere in the city. Shanahan remembered when there were only a few banks, and when their presence didn't scream out like an all-night diner. The law offices reflected the architect's original intent, more subdued, stiff but modest, much like Mrs Fournier's home.

Shanahan recognized the sturdy Margaret Tice,

who ran the Second Chance Community Center. She dressed for the occasion. She wore a navy blue suit, but still looked like she might have come in from the potato field. She nodded noncommittally in the direction of Shanahan and Bailey. Next to her was a small-framed black gentleman in an ill-fitting suit, sitting with his back to the window. He and Jennifer Bailey exchanged quick and cold looks when she came in. From then on, there were only stolen glances. He moved his eyes but not his head.

His name, Shanahan learned when introductions were made, was Charles Bailey, brother of Jennifer and of the deceased.

No daughter. No one inquired about her absence.

The attorney waited a moment before proceeding. He then opened the large manila envelope and pulled out a thick loose-leaf notebook with several tabs.

'All beneficiaries will be given a hard copy and a CD of the contents of the trust and will. This is a revised document that was finalized late last month. You remain executor of the will, Miss Bailey; however, certain responsibilities have been transferred to your brother, Charles.'

Jennifer Bailey blinked. Otherwise, she gave away nothing. Charles stole a glance. Margaret Tice seemed deep in thought.

'I want to know where he goes,' Shanahan said, walking toward the Lexus. Charles Bailey went south on Meridian toward the circle. 'How long was your brother in prison?' Shanahan opened the car door for her.

'Follow that man in the brown suit, Harold,' she said. 'But don't let him know it. I don't want him disappearing.' She took a deep breath, before saying in a soft growl, 'Until it's time for him to disappear.'

She settled in. 'Most of his life,' she said, addressing Shanahan's question. 'He'd pop out from time to time, promise to go straight. One or both of us would stake him some money . . .' She smiled, closed her eyes. 'Charles is a confidence man. It's his nature. I came to this conclusion before Alexandra. Obviously.'

'What's his line?'

'Survival. Whatever it takes. He used to be violent. Armed robbery. Later, he changed strategy. His line is what we used to call "bunko."'

'How do you figure he got your sister to let him in like that?'

She shook her head 'no' again and again. 'You'll find out, won't you?'

And there it was. Out of the blue. The estranged brother returns in time to benefit from his sister's death.

Charles got into a plain Nissan, a rental. Harold slowed, pulled into a vacant space next to a fire hydrant and waited for the prey to pull out, and if they were lucky, he'd go to the place he called home rather than, say, an afternoon movie.

Shanahan noticed that Harold's ear bud was not fully pushed in. Was he worried he wouldn't hear Jennifer Bailey's instructions? Or did he want to make sure he could pick up the conversation? Was he being protective or too curious?

Charles went around Monument Circle, where

major east–west and north–south corridors intersected. One could go round and round forever. Charles, a cautious fellow, went around three times before doubling back, taking Meridian to 38th Street, and then 38th out to Shadeland Avenue and Pendleton Pike, eventually ending up in a cheap motel. The front of the building looked decent. The rooms were behind a concrete block structure that should have reminded Charles Fournier of prison. They waited a moment. Shanahan walked around back. There, among a battered pickup and a hand-painted, shark-finned Cadillac convertible was the Nissan, parked in front of number 107.

'Are you going to talk to him?' Jennifer Bailey asked.

'I'll need to talk to you first.'

She instructed Harold to take her home. They went by a strip mall, a Dunkin' Donuts and a liquor store, more than enough and probably a desirable selection for a man who spent much of his time behind bars in Michigan City.

'You are the executor, yet you didn't have a copy of the most recent documents?'

'No, I didn't. I had what Alexandra gave me four years ago. She had it drawn up shortly after her husband died. I didn't think any more of it.'

'What's the difference?'

'My copy lists Tyrus Investments among the assets. The new one doesn't.'

'What does that mean?'

'I'm not sure. Apparently she owned it and whatever it is, or was, it's not coming to me as initially intended. I knew all major cash and assets would be allocated to the Center. But this strange Tyrus Investments was to come to me. However, it appears she split it out and gave it to Charles. He ran a con on her,' Bailey said, baring her prosecuting attorney persona.

'What makes you think that?'

'His look when I asked. The attorney knew nothing, but Charles did. Ever since he was a kid, I could see right through him. That's why he went to Alexandra.'

'Why didn't you know?'

'There's only two months between the drawing of the first trust, the copy I had, and the one read today.'

'Different law firms?'

'Yes,' Jennifer Bailey said. 'She didn't tell me she re-did it or that she talked with Charles.'

'What's Tyrus?'

'I don't know. I asked her when she gave me that first copy. She said I'd know when I needed to know.'

Bailey seemed to want a little solitude, perhaps to sort things out. Shanahan went outside. Harold stood by the car.

Shanahan asked if they could stop for lunch.

'You're the boss,' Harold said.

'MCL.'

'Over on Arlington?'

'That's the one.'

It was a short trip. Harold backed into the parking space.

'Can I buy you lunch?' Shanahan asked.

'Brought my own.' Harold held up a brown bag.

'Be good tomorrow, won't it? You'll be ahead of the game.'

'I'm good.'

'This isn't a black and white thing, is it?'

'A you and me thing,' Harold said.

'Good. I'm used to that.' Shanahan opened the car door and started to get out, changed his mind. 'Why didn't she let you do the investigating? She's already bought your time.'

'You're not as dumb as I thought,' Harold said. But it didn't change anything. He stayed put.

MCL was a small cafeteria, homey except for the steam table set in the midst of an aluminum cave. He ordered the turkey and dressing, mashed potatoes, sweet potatoes and peas. He also picked up a plate of biscuits. At the cashier, he pulled out a twenty from his wallet after fumbling and dropping it once. A small scrap of paper fell on his tray.

'Do you want help with your tray?' the cashier asked.

'No.' He didn't wonder why people found him unfriendly. His 'no' came out like a warning. Truth was he could carry the tray. He might not be able to operate his left hand, and he had the broken plates to prove it, but once it got hold of something, the grip was solid as a vice. It was also hard to let go.

He found a small table and arranged his lunch, putting the tray on another table. He looked at the note, the pencil scribbles.

'Damn,' he said, loud enough to turn heads. It

was the address he found in Alexandra Fournier's purse. He forgot he had it. He hadn't followed up nor had he turned it over to the police. There was no question. He was slipping. Seriously slipping.

He had overestimated his hunger.

'That was quick,' Harold said, stuffing half a sandwich back into the bag.

Shanahan handed him the address.

'And then let's go talk to Charles.'

The address was on 10th. All they had to do was pull out of the lot and turn left and they'd be on their way, descending from a modest, well-kept middle-class neighborhood – keeping its real estate value because of a golf course – to a run-down stretch and eventually to an area in the midst of abandonment.

There was nothing there. It was a parking lot. For what, Shanahan couldn't imagine. This wasn't a thriving retail center. Within a few blocks there were some gas stations, tire shops, liquor stores, and a place that billed itself, in pink neon, as a 'cocktail lounge.' Maybe the parking lot was merely a place to meet. No more significance than that.

Shanahan opted for the lounge. He motioned his intentions to Harold, who communicated he understood by flashing the headlights.

'J.W. Dant and a Guinness,' Shanahan said to the guy wearing a Colts baseball cap and a sweatshirt. Shanahan believed that the death penalty should be reserved for guys over twenty who wore that kind of cap backward.

'You win the prize. Got neither of them,' the bartender said. 'You wanna go at it again?'

'Surprise me.' Shanahan sat.

He got a jigger of Jim Beam, a bottle of Heineken and very little information. Finally a tidbit: 'I pay my rent to Circle City Rental Management. Month to month.'

'Thirty-day notice? You afraid of being thrown out?'

'They're lucky to have me.'

'Doesn't make you insecure?'

'Life makes me insecure. Not much to do about it but roll with the punches. I'd be happy to sell if you're interested. We could work out a deal on the inventory, equipment, decor, goodwill.'

Shanahan looked around. 'Goodwill?'

'You'd be surprised what happens here on Saturday night.'

'Past my bed time.' He decided to change the subject. 'For Sale sign over by the parking lot. What do you know about that?'

'Yeah. New sign, old listing. Group of do gooders trying to spruce up the neighborhood. Made them put up a new sign.'

'Who's that?'

'I don't remember. A neighborhood group. Their big project is the restoration of the Rivoli Theater. Got some funding. Doubt if it will be enough.'

'And all the boarded-up buildings?' Shanahan asked, downing the shot. The heat felt good. It also took the edge off the stale smell of the 'cocktail lounge' in the afternoon. He took a heavy draw on the beer.

'Probably given up selling, just waiting for times to get better. Who is going to live that long?'

'Good point.' Shanahan looked at his watch.

The bartender smiled. 'You could do worse than die on a barstool.'

'Maybe I'll rent that one, over there by the door. I'll let you know.' He finished the beer.

Harold wore sunglasses today. He looked particularly formidable. Shanahan couldn't tell for sure, but he was likely carrying. He was the other day. Habit. One doesn't retire after thirty or more years with the state police without feeling naked without gun. Shanahan felt better knowing this because he was about to break into Charles' motel room. The rental car wasn't there and no one answered the knock. Still, it was important in this line of work not to make too many assumptions.

Charles was a neat kind of guy, which meant he might be more likely to know his domain had been searched. Maybe that would be a good thing. Make him nervous and more likely to make mistakes. Or make him run. Shanahan didn't want him to run, at least not quite yet.

Wrappers from a couple of fast food sandwiches, drinks and fries were stuffed into the sack, folded and put in a wastebasket. Last night, probably. The bed hadn't been made, but there had been an attempt to straighten out the blankets. Toiletries were store brands. Two prescription-pill containers. He recognized the names. Charles had arthritis serious enough to need beyond over-the-counter relief, and high blood pressure, despite his slight build, no doubt a family trait.

His suit was in the closet, carefully placed. There were two books on the bedside table, both by Chester Himes. There was a bookmark in one. It was a copy of a form Charles signed to acknowledge his receipt of a watch, a ring, a wallet, cell phone, keys and some cash when he was released from Michigan City. The date was four days before his sister was shot in the back of the head. Curious timing.

Stuck in the back of the book was a street map of Indianapolis. Several areas of the Eastside had been outlined. Shanahan wrote down the neighborhoods he identified and replaced the map. What was Charles Bailey doing? Plotting some sort of scam?

Shanahan's energy started to fade. He wanted to check in with homicide, check out anything with the word 'Tyrus' in it, the rental company the cocktail lounge paid its rent to and the real estate firm trying to sell the parking lot in a dying neighborhood. Phone work. He could do that from home. Computer work, if he belonged in today's world. Even so, Shanahan believed he had enough pieces to start making connections.

Twelve

They stood in Shanahan's front yard. The older detective had gathered a pitiful pile of leaves in an attempt to eventually get all of them before winter landed. He was giving lead homicide cop Collins just about everything he learned; except the map. Collins promised to track down when Charles Bailey was in and out of prison and any known associates, criminal or otherwise.

'Anything new on Leonard Card?' Shanahan asked.

'Trying to stay invisible until after the hearing. Word is that those who brought the charges are backing off.'

'Why?'

Collins shrugged. 'Why are you interested?'

'Alexandra Fournier was on the committee.'

'So are thirteen other people. And they have more than a few other cops under the microscope.' Collins looked down the lawn to the patch of green that hid the shooter that morning. 'I'll find out more. I don't know. If we find a connection between Card and Charles, who knows? I can check Card's cases.'

'I'll catch you later,' Shanahan said, heading back to the house.

'Shanahan,' Collins called out. 'I'm playing a little fast and loose with you and the murder investigation. I can't imagine what they'd think if you were caught meddling in the police oversight committee case.'

'You mean "we," don't you?'

'Oh yeah, a big, dead "we."'

Shanahan had already called Circle City Rental Management and Crossroads Real Estate. The rental company did what rental companies do: managed property for out-of-town landlords, for estates or for people who simply didn't want to be bothered with the day-to-day business. Crossroads provided nothing. They had more questions than answers and neither knew of a company called Tyrus Investments. Information had no phone number for them.

Shanahan plied Maureen with a rum and tonic and reservations for dinner at the Black Market, a trendy restaurant Maureen had been begging to try and Shanahan was trying to avoid. Tonight, he thought, was the perfect time and a fine, expensive restaurant the perfect place.

'So, I'm going to have to sing for my supper?' Maureen asked.

'I thought I was being subtle.'

'You always think you're being subtle.'

'How else could I have gotten where I am today?'

'And where are you?'

'Sitting across the dinner table from the most beautiful woman in the world.'

'You call that subtle?'

'Well?'

'I'll take it. What do you need from me?'

'Rental management companies. Legit business?'

'Same as others. The people who build or own office parks or apartment buildings may not have the resources to manage them. Maintenance, vacancies, evictions, rent collection.'

'Crossroads Real Estate. Have you heard of them?'

Maureen paused a moment. 'Yes, kind of a bargain basement brand.'

'What does that mean?'

'Let's say Madonna wanted to move to Indianapolis, she'd call your girlfriend, Regina.'

'Regina?'

'Regina Thompkins. Remember, your girlfriend who works for a hotsy-totsy real estate firm. She knows the expensive market, homes most people don't even know are for sale. Crossroads is at the other end. They have properties that have been on the market for decades. They specialize in foreclosures, fixer-uppers, and lots in rundown neighborhoods.'

'How do they make any money?'

'No overhead, no staff. Just a long, long list. Law of averages means something on that list will sell sometime.'

'Tyrus Investments.'

There was a long pause. 'Nothing,' she said. 'Never heard of it.'

Dinner interrupted the interrogation. Shanahan had already finished half his glass of Floyd's Gumballhead beer, brewed in Munster, Indiana and was about to order a bottle of Founders Double Trouble from Grand Rapids, Michigan when his flat- iron steak arrived. Maureen looked lovingly at her plate of fried perch and corn waffles.

The crowd was certainly younger, many of them sharing great, long tables. It was a happy, trendy place serving brewpub beer and such delicacies as roasted marrow bones and something called a beef tongue cocktail. Sides included collard greens and grits.

'What do you think?' Shanahan asked, looking around.

'Love it,' she said. 'I'm surprised. Thank you.'

'So is this the wave of the future?'

'What do you mean?'

'For this area? Is the Eastside movin' on up?'

'You're asking me this as a real estate agent?'

'Would I be wise to buy property, let's say on Tenth Street? This area seems to be blossoming.'

'No. You'd never see a return.'

'Too old?'

'Yes. You're not really . . .'

'No.' He explained his fuzzy concept as best he could. There was another neighborhood buried beneath the debris of urban decay of East 10th Street. Not only was Irvington just a few miles east but here was more. Old architecture that, if not harvested soon, would be in ruins. There was a movie theater amid the boarded-up stores and there was Woodruff Place, an incredibly grand old neighborhood with grand old homes in various stages of upkeep. Three long, wide streets, each separated by grassy islands with mature trees, quaint turnarounds for buggies and

74

later, cars. In the center of each turnaround was a fountain. This was the setting for the classic Booth Tarkington novel and Orson Welles's film, *The Magnificent Ambersons*. History on top of history.

'With the proper management and a plethora of grants, subsidies and tax exemptions, this part of town could take a giant leap into desirability,' Shanahan said.

Fortunes could be made. And there were reputations to be built by the young and aspiring.

Shanahan finished his draft and sipped from the newly arrived bottle. Talking about it made it seem more viable.

Tenth Street also ran into Massachusetts Avenue, where they dined at the moment with the city's future leaders. And Massachusetts Avenue was adjacent to downtown, which was enjoying its own rejuvenation, shopping, restaurants, new hotels and sport stadiums. There were already quaint and charming historic districts housing – high-quality renovations for the newly wealthy – in Lockerbie and Chatham Arch.

'I'm impressed,' she said.

'So?'

'So, look how long it took for Mass Avenue to take root. Look at Fountain Square. It sits there begging for this kind of development. Not much is happening. If there were a lot of property changing hands on the Eastside, I'd know something about it. Irvington is pretty hot, but where you are looking, nothing. And that whole area. It's huge. There is a movement toward urban living. It's becoming fashionable and it's also efficient. It's also slow. The city is working on mass transit with some seriousness. How did you come up with all this?'

'The sisters have a brother, Charles, the con man. He apparently worked his more gullible sister to give him something called Tyrus Investments.'

Maureen nodded.

'I checked his current dwelling and found nothing helpful except an Indianapolis street map that had the areas I've mentioned to you outlined as if they formed something united.'

'You think Tyrus and this map are connected?'

'I don't have much more than that. I have a dirty cop who is on the verge of losing his pension and a very unsuccessful criminal who wants one last con to take him into his golden years. Each has ties to the victim.'

'How about to each other?' Maureen asked.

Maureen brought her laptop to bed. Maureen and Shanahan took the satellite-view tour outlined on Charles' printed map. The more they looked at it the more it made sense. It could work, but as Maureen reminded him, Indianapolis's power players weren't noted for great leaps in creative thinking. On the other hand, he reminded himself, Charles could use this kind of pie-in-the-sky plan connection to the mysterious Tyrus Investments to run some sort of scam, independent of anything real or even possible. It occurred to him that at the reading, Charles received nothing else. Nothing in terms of tangible assets, nothing even sentimental. If Alexandra had bad feelings toward her brother, how did he get Tyrus? Shanahan would have a serious talk with the man. Even Margaret Tice, the overseer of the Second Chance Community Center, personally received $10,000 from Alexandra's trust. Perhaps they had been close. He would have a serious talk with her.

So there it was: he slipped out of the bed, putting on hold Maureen's guided tour of the city's other eastside. He called Bailey to set up a meeting with the former state attorney general and her wayward brother. He didn't think she'd like the idea. He was wrong, but she did have a condition. Jennifer Bailey wanted a sit-down with her brother in the morning – and not at her home.

'I don't want that bloodsucker anywhere near my home,' she said. 'Bloodsucker' sounded positively obscene coming from her. 'You and Harold can see to that, can't you?'

'We'll need to do it early so he doesn't get away.'

'Harold will pick you up at six,' she said.

'We're here, near the entrance to Woodruff Place. Let's take a trip down Middle Drive,' Maureen said when Shanahan returned. Illuminated by the gold light of the bedside table lamp. Shanahan knew that whatever damage time was doing to his body and mind, he was one lucky guy. She turned the laptop screen toward him. 'We can park under this tree.'

Harold backed the Lexus into a space along a chain-link fence, kept the engine running. The Nissan rental was parked by the door. Shanahan knocked. He looked around. The early morning light was thin. He knocked again. Cars and trucks could be heard on the Pike.

Charles, skinny and frail in his white boxers, was confused and angry.

'What do you want?'

Shanahan noted he didn't ask who Shanahan was, but what he wanted. Who Shanahan was and what he was doing at the reading wasn't explained at the time.

'Your sister wants to talk with you,' Shanahan said stepping to the back of the room to make sure he was right that there was no exit.

Charles followed for a few steps before coming back to the front, screaming, 'She's not coming here. She can't come in here.' He looked around. He was in a panic.

'You two don't like each other.'

'She's not human.'

'That's a little harsh,' Shanahan said. 'Get dressed.'

'You're nothin' to me,' Charles said.

Shanahan walked to the door, motioned for Harold. The big man got out of the car, a bit unhappy about doing Shanahan's bidding. It was a frustrating, sulking, and intimidating kind of walk. It was effective.

'OK, anywhere, not here.'

Shanahan met Harold before he got to the door. 'If you would, call Miss Bailey, pick her up and we'll meet at my place.'

'How are you getting around?'

'I'm sure Charles will give me a lift.'

Charles did object but agreed when he was told his only other choice was to ride with Harold.

Shanahan noticed a dark something – a small truck or a large car – pull out just as Charles made a left from the drive in front of the motel and another on to Shadeland. The shadow vehicle followed them onto Shadeland before disappearing. Maybe they only dropped back, which would suggest a pro. Then again, maybe he was imagining things.

Thirteen

'What brings you back to Indianapolis?' Shanahan asked as Charles kept looking at the speedometer.

'Everybody's got to be somewhere.'

'This somewhere hasn't been very kind to you. Yet you come back. And this time you come back just a few days before your sister is murdered.'

'I'm not a lucky guy.'

'Luckier than your sister.'

'You've got a mouth on you.'

'Turn right on Sixteenth.'

'Kidnapping is a federal crime,' Charles said.

'Tell me about Tyrus,' Shanahan said.

'What? Don't know what you're talking about.'

'If you didn't know what I was talking about, you would have asked "who" not "what."'

The neighborhood was improving. CVS Pharmacy, a Wendy's on the corner. Chains still, but well kept. Soon they moved onto Pleasant Run, where commerce gave way to time stopped in the thirties or forties, solid homes embedded in timeless nature.

They pulled into the driveway. Shanahan grabbed the car keys, got out and surveyed the area for the tail. He didn't see anything suspicious, and a sniper wouldn't have had time to set up.

Maureen met them at the door.

'This is Charles,' Shanahan said. 'Charles, Maureen.'

Charles nodded, followed her inside.

'Coffee?' she asked.

He nodded again.

'When he gets his voice back,' Shanahan said, 'he's going to tell us all about Tyrus.'

Maureen disappeared into the kitchen. Charles sat at one end of the sofa. Maureen had a fire going.

Charles spoke, still not looking up. 'I'm not a nice guy. You figured that out, right?'

'We're on the same page here.'

'So the only reason I'm telling you is because of my safety, not yours. You've become a pest. Not to me, I don't give a shit. But I suspect pest control has been called. You get my meaning?' For the first time he looked at Shanahan, right into his eyes. 'I don't want to be caught up in that whole extermination thing. You know what I'm sayin'?'

Maureen came in balancing three mugs of coffee. Quiet descended on the space. Shanahan had no more questions because it was clear Charles wasn't giving out answers.

The ambiance changed when Jennifer Bailey arrived with the hefty Harold behind her. The silence turned heavy.

Shanahan, Maureen and finally Harold – though he hovered at the edge, eyes on Charles – migrated to the kitchen as the sound level rose. It was a good idea. Charles, defending himself from his dominating and shrill older sister, gave up what he had tried so hard to hide.

'Easy for you, princess,' Charles said. 'You were given everything. An education, the best clothes, a car.'

'You eliminated a university education with your poor grades and behavior in high school. They were prepared to do the same for you as they did for Alexandra and me.'

'I was the stray dog with fleas from the time I was born . . .'

'You were a devious little scoundrel from the get-go.'

'Yes, there!' he shouted. 'From the get-go. When my life was formed, I was made out to be a criminal. And even later, when I came to you for help, some little bit of assistance to get my life on track, you refused. Your cold, brittle heart was closed.'

'I helped. Many times. To find you work, but you just wanted it the easy way. Money, which you'd lose and then commit another crime, get caught and lose more years of your life. That's why you went to Alexandra. She was a sucker for sad stories and you could wear that sad face and get what you wanted.'

'She was blood. She had a heart. She understood me. She knew that this time, I would work. I'd be on my way, no burden on anyone, a success. Alexandra wanted that for me.'

'That why you killed her?'

'I didn't kill her. If I was gonna kill a relative you gotta know who that would be.'

'You saw her before she died,' she said. 'Few days, in fact.'

'I did. A visit. I was here on business and

ready to start my new life. I wanted to thank her.'

Jennifer was as sharp as ever, Shanahan thought. She had pieced the puzzle together as far as the known pieces allowed.

'Charles, I have a copy of her trust, the one she made out shortly after Halston died. Listed in the assets was something called Tyrus Investments. Mere months after that she went to a different attorney, drew up another legal document, which superseded the first, in which there is no mention of Tyrus. As I recall, you were between sentences at the time. You tried to hit me up for some investment having to do with solar heating. We were going to talk about it, but you never followed up. You went to Alexandra, didn't you?'

'I don't remember. It was long ago.'

'She didn't want me to see the new will.'

'She knew you'd throw a fit, didn't she?' Charles said, the tone childish.

'She knew I'd put a stop to it and you knew I'd check out this Tyrus business.'

'What she knew is that you have a cold and unforgiving heart. Look at you. You spent your life punishing people. She spent her life helping them.'

'Only four years, Charles, enough time for the mysterious Tyrus Investments to disappear just as you did. And now you reappear at the reading. Why? Maybe she had something else for you? She didn't, did she? In fact, she learned something that put your plan in jeopardy. You also wanted to make sure you caught all this in time and she hadn't changed the will again. Fortunately for you she didn't have time. You made sure of that, didn't you? Harold!' she yelled.

He followed her out of the door.

'Mr Shanahan and I and the police will finish up pretty soon,' she said, stopping briefly. 'You'll fry, this time.'

The living room was quiet again. Maureen went to the bedroom. Charles sat, all huddled into himself.

'I didn't kill my sister,' Charles said.

'I know. But it doesn't matter,' Shanahan said. 'We can wrap all this up so that it looks that way. Motive, opportunity. Look at your past, Charles. Armed robbery. Miss Bailey is happy. Maybe I get a bonus for delivering you to death row.'

Charles stood slowly. Shanahan tossed him the keys to the rental, then turned away, picked up the phone, dialed his own number, waited a moment. 'Homicide please, Captain Collins.' He went to the window, watched as Charles backed out.

Shanahan's conversation with Collins was brief.

'You think he killed his sister?' Maureen asked.

'No.' Shanahan set the phone down. 'He has serious arthritis. Alexandra was shot by a skilled professional, a trained sniper, not someone who once robbed a Seven-Eleven with a thirty-eight.'

The phone sounded.

'Hello,' he said.

'How did I do?' Miss Bailey said.

* * *

84

She sent Harold back. The day was young. Shanahan wished he were. It was back out to see Margaret Tice. While it might be interesting to see who showed up for the funeral service, likely a large crowd, the only people at the intimate reading beside the attorney and himself were family, such as it was, and Margret Tice. And the family didn't get along. Tice appeared to be the only person who knew anything of Alexandra Fournier's business.

'Do we have anything to make a sandwich out of?' Shanahan asked, eyes scouring the refrigerator for something interesting and easy.

'You know as much as I do.'

'Not about sandwiches.' He rooted through the refrigerator.

'Peanut butter,' she said.

'I'm too old for peanut butter.'

'That's foolish.'

'Proves my point. Egg sandwich,' he said. 'Goddamn egg sandwich.' He looked at his watch.

'Your pills,' she said, bringing him a little saucer of variously colored pills.

Margaret Tice's dresses all seemed to be cut the same way. Even at the reading, a bit of bosom showed. Fabric tightened over butt and thighs. It was short-sleeved despite the increasingly chilly weather.

Shanahan remembered that most of the kids at Second Chance were at school in the mornings and afternoons; there were a few children in the recreation room. The television was on and loud.

Shanahan guided her outside. Across the street were the vacant lots destined to be urban farmland.

'How often did Alexandra come down here?'

'Every day.'

'Did she get visitors?'

'Sometimes. Potential donors. People from other places trying to duplicate what she was doing here.'

'The Center already own that land?'

'Yes. That was the last of it.'

'What do you mean "the last of it"?'

'It was from her husband before he died. He had an option on it and Alexandra cashed it in shortly after the judge died. It was his real estate savvy that got us this,' she said, hand sweeping to indicate the entire center. 'Some are trades or what not.'

'I see. Her brother come to see her here?'

'Yeah. Not for years, then a few days ago.'

'Nice, civil chat?'

'No. And she was real frustrated when they parted.'

'She tell you anything about the conversation?'

'No.'

'She ever tell you anything about him?'

'She said he was the "white sheep" of the family. She thought that was funny.'

'The $10,000 to you, personally. You must have been good friends.'

'She wasn't someone you got close to. But she knew I cared about the center. She appreciated that.'

86

'What will happen now?'

'Operationally the center can run for a few years. And I can manage it for a long time if the board wants. But I'm not Alexandra. I don't have the community standing or fundraising skills. I can balance the books but I can't get rich people to write checks. I'm hoping I can get the board to find someone. Maybe Alexandra's sister.'

'She have any other visitors, especially lately?'

'No.'

'Anything suspicious you noticed in the last few weeks or days leading up to her death?'

'I don't think so. Well, maybe. There was an unmarked police car hanging around.'

'How'd you know it was police if it was unmarked?'

'Everybody knew. The kids knew. He wasn't fooling anyone. You know these unmarked cars don't fool anybody.'

He knew.

'You didn't find that strange?' he asked.

'Not at all. Some of the kids here are never far from the streets. The world out there offers a lot of temptation. The sirens,' she said with a tiny smile.

'Was Mrs Fournier the same during those days that led up to . . .'

'Maybe a little distracted the day before. But it's hard to tell with her. She was so organized, it was a little crazy.'

'What do you mean?'

'Everything was always scheduled with her. If it was Tuesday, she'd have a tuna fish sandwich. She had a standing hair appointment on the

87

fifteenth. She washed her car on Saturday. She signed checks on the twenty-fifth of every month. Everything was like that. She was chained to the calendar and to the clock.'

'Where to?' Harold asked as Shanahan climbed into the back seat.

'Time for lunch, don't you think?'

'Could be. Your call, boss.'

'Ellenberger Park.'

'Ellenberger. There's no restaurant over there.'

'Got my own brown bag today. We can enjoy lunch together.'

'That's sweet,' Harold said.

'Park under a big old tree. Talk about old times.'

'It's a cinch there won't be that many new times,' Harold said.

'I know. I see three tubes of toothpaste on sale for fifty percent off at Walgreens. And I can't be sure I'll live long enough to benefit from the bargain.'

Harold laughed. 'Live dangerously, Mr Shanahan. Don't be afraid of green bananas.'

'Not a choice anymore.'

Fourteen

The park had lost its green to the sudden frost of a few weeks previous and was half-naked. Shanahan used to walk his dog, Casey, over the gentle rolling hills. In the summer one could hear the shouts of children in the pool. In the winter, in the snow, the world was dead silent. An oddly comforting deadly silence.

'Did the sisters visit each other often?'

'Ask your client,' Harold said.

'I like to get different points of view.'

'If you think I'm going to talk about Miss Bailey behind her back, you're sorely mistaken.'

'I'm not trying to get you to reveal any deep, dark secrets.'

'She's not paying you to investigate her.'

'She is, Harold.'

'How does that work?'

'People don't always know about themselves, how others regard them, for example. You may think you're someone's friend and you are an enemy. Maybe you stand in the way of what someone wants and you don't know it.'

Harold twisted off the cap to his thermos. 'Maybe she did it herself.'

'Maybe. It's got to be considered.'

'Are you for real?'

'I have to look into it,' Shanahan said.

'Why would she hire you if she thought it would lead back to her?'

'Maybe she thought if she hired a feeble old PI with brain damage, I'd never figure it out, but she'd look like she was the loyal, leave-no-stone-unturned sister.'

'I'll go along with the first part of your scenario.'

'What I really believe is that Miss Bailey wants people to think that Charles did it. And she wants him to pay for it.'

'Do you think he did it?'

'No. He's not steady enough to get her at that distance. And he's not strong enough to strangle a seventeen-year-old kid.'

'But he knows stuff,' Harold said.

'He does,' Shanahan said. 'Now, you are strong enough,' Shanahan said. 'And with your special combat training, you could have pulled the trigger.'

'You flatter me. It's been a lot of years.'

'Some things you don't forget. And you've held up pretty well.'

'My motive?'

'She wanted you to.'

'Her motive?'

'Money. Kill her before she gave everything away. Alexandra stole the judge from her. He made the pile of money. Now, Charles is back and he's walking away with part of that pile in the form of Tyrus Investments.'

'Why would I help her?'

Shanahan wasn't sure he wanted to answer that but he did.

'Money. And maybe you're in love with her.'

90

'Is this how your story ends?' Harold asked.

'Not necessarily. I'm just answering your question about why I'd investigate the person who hired me. My job is to find out who did it. We go wherever the evidence leads.'

'I'll be damned,' Harold said. 'I got another question for you. What do we do now?'

'I think we've given Charles enough time to stew. Let's find out some stuff.'

'All this freedom, and you're in a motel room,' Shanahan said at the doorway of Room 107.

'Crazy, isn't it?' Charles said. 'And I still got a bug bangin' at the screen.'

'Could be worse. Why don't we go inside? Someone could die out here.'

'Won't break my heart,' Charles said.

'I don't mean me. You've become an extraneous, embarrassing detail.'

Charles blinked a couple of times, bowed his head and stepped back into the room.

'What do you think you know?' he asked, shutting the door behind Shanahan, squeezing all but the slightest light from the room.

The question was perfect. But Shanahan's question was risky. If Charles knew how little Shanahan knew, the con would simply shut down.

'You've already signed over the options, right?'

Charles bowed his head again. Shanahan realized it wasn't that this tic was a way to keep from seeing, but to keep from being seen. Charles's hands involuntarily clenched.

'Go away,' Charles said.

'We have lots to talk about, Charles. Tyrus Investments. Murder.'

Charles got up, threw a duffel bag on the bed and began to stuff his meager belongings inside.

'Have you got your cut?'

Charles acted like he was alone in the room.

'Did you know your sister was going to get it?'

'It's her fault, not mine. They don't know when to let things go.'

'Your sisters?'

'Just let things go and nothing would happen.'

'Your sister Jennifer too?' Shanahan asked.

'What do you think?'

'You're going to get her killed too?'

'That's the way she is.'

'You the middle kid?' Shanahan asked.

'The youngest.'

'They're both tough women, your sisters.'

Charles laughed. It was unguarded and charming.

'I was a talker, talked myself into and out of trouble. I couldn't get very far with Jenny. But Alex, that's a different story. Her mind was ruled by her heart. She was a sucker for a sob story, especially if you had a plan to change your life.'

'You had a plan, didn't you?'

Charles's smile slipped away. 'Gotta have a plan.'

'You think you're home free? You're involved in a murder.'

'Ain't so,' Charles said. 'Anyways, what are you? Not the law. Not a big-time bad guy. What have you got?'

'Something,' Shanahan said. 'You're moving pretty quick to get out of here.'

92

'Your visiting ain't helping me out any. You know what I'm saying. Alex was at your front door, wasn't she?' Charles said, an accusation more than implied.

He laughed, took the Bible from the bedside table, tossed it into the bag.

'And Mr Smartass Know-it-all . . . you too. We're all gonna do the dance now. People can't mind their own fucking business.'

He nearly knocked Shanahan over, heading to the door. Shanahan followed. Charles dropped his bag, felt all his pockets, went back inside, no doubt for his car keys. Shanahan waited for him.

'You could stop all of this,' Shanahan said.

He felt something sting his ear. He saw a red dot appear on Charles' forehead.

Harold, 9mm drawn, was there in a second. He looked in the only direction the shot could have come from. So did Shanahan. Nothing to see. There was a two-story building close enough for a skillful sniper to do his work and far enough away to come and go without being seen.

Shanahan raised his hand to his ear. He found some blood.

'It's nothing,' Harold said. 'Don't worry.'

'Get back to your boss, Harold. We don't know who is next.'

'What about you?'

'I'll go inside, call the police. The shooter is gone. For now.'

'You're kind of a bad luck charm, aren't you?' Captain Collins asked.

'You might not want to stand too close.'

93

'What are you doing here?' Collins asked.

'Delivering the magic word.'

'And that is?'

'Options.'

'Tell me more,' Collins said. Behind him investigators were doing their work. Swann was there, doing the hands-on supervising.

'Maybe "Tyrus Investments."'

'We did a search on that when you first mentioned it. What did we get? Squat.'

'What we have are murders by a professional killer. We have a mysterious entity called "Tyrus" that involved both victims. And all I know is that Charles nearly went into shock when I mentioned the word "options." That's the secret word that leads to the treasure or doom.'

'Interesting take. You said both victims. There was a third. Nicky Hernandez.' Collins looked him in the eye.

'Wrong place. Wrong time,' Shanahan said, though he wasn't comfortable lumping them together.

'Would seem so,' Collins said. 'A versatile hitman, though, don't you think?'

Collins hadn't bought the threesome either.

Fifteen

'What happened?' Maureen asked when she came home from work and found him mixing her a rum and tonic. Her eyes were focused on the Band-Aid on his ear.

'I cut myself shaving.'

'You shave your ears?'

'You don't know the half of it.'

She gave him the 'don't-be-stupid' look.

'The sniper killed Charles.'

'And your ear was in the way?'

'That sums it up pretty well. How about a funeral tomorrow?'

'It wasn't on my wish list.' She took the drink. 'This was.'

'Miss Bailey is going to need Harold. She not only has her sister's service, but arrangements for her brother.'

'Wow.' Maureen shook her head. 'And then there was one.'

'End of the line.'

'And you need a ride?' Maureen sipped her drink.

'I need a protector. I haven't been in a church in quite a while.'

'You're afraid of retribution. Or the Devil.'

'You can beat the Devil.'

'Let me check. What time?' She retrieved her laptop.

Shanahan went to the sofa, sat beside her. She marked her place in a Megan Abbott book.

'Do you think we need a tuffett?'

She smiled, set the book aside. 'Are you offering curds and whey?'

'If you will answer one question.'

'That's from a different fairy tale.'

'Options?' he asked.

She looked confused. 'I guess we can go right to sleep, talk about the meaning of life, or mess around if . . .'

'Property options. How do they work?'

'I'm not at that level, Shanahan. When people come to me, they either want to buy a house or sell one. Nothing complicated. And, for the most part, not commercial property. I really don't know my way around the business world. I'm sure there are people in the property investment business and I'd guess an option would work the way they do with stocks. You agree to buy a certain amount of stock before a certain time at a set amount, no matter what the market is at that moment. You could probably do the same with property.'

The fire wasn't all the way out. There were some burning embers and an occasional flare up.

Kowalski was complaining not so much about the hour of Shanahan's call, but that this was Kowalski's time set for play and not 'legal crap,' especially the 'infinitely boring contract law.'

'Humor me,' Shanahan said.

'Can't be any simpler.'

'Pretend I'm in the third grade.'

'Good. Then you'll get it in thirty seconds. It's all contract law. I'll give you something if you give me something. When we agree on the some-things, we write it down and we both sign it. We get it notarized. Shazam, we have a contract. We don't file anything. We don't get anybody's approval.'

'All done in secret?'

'Certainly can be. You want to know why someone would want an option to buy?'

'Right,' Shanahan said.

'Rather than just buy it?'

'Right again.'

'You alluded to one of them. Sales of property are disclosed. People will know. Secondly, an option usually favors the purchaser, since he is not required to exercise it. Most likely the buyer puts down a small amount compared to the eventual purchase price – an amount he is prepared to lose. Let's say the buyer thinks the property will be worth a million in five years. Maybe he knows something about future development in the area. He gives the property owner $10,000 for the option and agrees to pay $500,000 in five years. As time goes on, somebody puts the kibosh on the proposed development. Suddenly the future doesn't look so bright. The option holder decides to pass on the purchase. He's only out $10,000, not $500,000. And nobody knows he was a fool. Essentially, this is what bankers do with your savings account these days. It's a form of gambling.'

Shanahan was surprised he understood what Kowalski was saying.

'Could someone sell their option?' Shanahan asked. 'Or group of options?'

'It's a contract, Shanahan. Paramount could buy a movie star's contract from MGM. Baseball teams do it all the time with players. Do what you want. Any two people can enter into a contract about pretty much anything. For a dollar and a half you may use my umbrella, but only on Thursdays if it starts to rain after three p.m. Sign here.'

'Thanks,' Shanahan said. 'I owe you dinner.'

'Listen, at this time of night you need to be making love or drinking a fine liquor, listening to Coltrane or asleep dreaming of a planet with a tribe of long-legged women with three breasts. Not talking about options.'

'I've been remiss,' Shanahan said, disconnecting.

The fire had gone. Maureen had disappeared. She was in the bedroom. In bed.

He could relax. Maureen's breaths were long and deep. He thought about all the hoopla he'd attend the next day. If he knew of a way to miss a funeral, any funeral, Shanahan would. Maureen felt the same way. He was going, not to pay his respects, but to see who was there and possibly catch them off guard. He had more questions. Maureen was going as collaborator, chauffeur and, primarily, as an observer. A spy.

Shanahan took advantage of Maureen's deep sleep in the morning. Toast, coffee, the newspaper, the morning news on television. Otherwise, space and time were quiet and still.

Autumn had settled in outside. As if to remind the elderly PI of that fact as well as his need to

98

do some gutter cleaning and lawn raking, a gold leaf fluttered down slow enough for its fall to be noticed.

Both the newspaper and local TV news were focused on the series of murders. The consensus was that the deaths of Alexandra and Charles were connected, likely a 'family' thing. Nicky Hernandez was a fluke, they implied. Wrong time. Wrong place. A witness to a break in. The reporters alluded to how little the police had provided them with. Shanahan noticed that no mention was made of the fact that brother and sister were killed by a sniper. The police probably held this back as a way to root out false confessions or decide between more than one suspect. But much was made of the fact that prior to Alexandra's death her office was tossed by an intruder, who, upon being discovered, must have killed the person who saw him and, a short time later, killed Alexandra. The police confirmed they were looking for one killer, though they fell short of any indication there was a person of interest for that role.

Police also kept Shanahan's name out of the news, referring to him as a 'retired gentleman recovering from serious surgery'. They did it because they didn't want him – a loose cannon at best – mucking up the investigation. As far as Shanahan was concerned, he couldn't have asked for a better arrangement. He didn't want to have to deal with the press unless they proved useful.

The Eastern Star Baptist Church was not what he had expected. Instead of a small church with a relatively solid turnout of supporters from her expanded community, the place was huge, and yet still filled with thousands of well-dressed attendees. The lighting was extensive and professional. The stage could have accommodated *Oklahoma* or *Porgy and Bess*.

The parking lot should have hinted at the contents.

'Goodness,' Maureen said.

Mrs Thompkins was there in black. She talked with Mr Holcomb, who wore black Armani. Thompkins touched him on the shoulder and whispered in his ear. They weren't the only white faces, but among the few. Mrs Tice sat close to the stage. She stared ahead. Eventually Shanahan located Captain Collins, who had the charisma of a movie star. He was scanning the crowd as well. Shanahan looked for the attorney who read the will or trust or whatever it was. He found himself standing beside Holcomb instead.

'No stone unturned?' Holcomb asked Shanahan.

'I could ask the same of you. As I understand it, you and Mrs Fournier weren't on the same page with regard to Leonard Card.'

'I have no idea if that is true. The committee does not yet have all the information. It's true that she was a little more spirited in her questions regarding Officer Card.'

'You were more reticent than Thompkins, the law-and-order candidate. That's odd. Aren't you afraid you'll disappoint your constituency?'

'If by that you mean the black community, you might be a victim of stereotypes. Black families want to see the end of violence in their

100

communities. They want the police to be tough. We can't expect to clean up the neighborhoods if we micromanage the police and punish those on the front lines.'

'At the expense of innocent young men?'

'The jury is out on Card. Crime is down in the neighborhood.'

There was a moment of quiet, heads turned to the rear. The silence dissipated into a chorus of indistinguishable whispers. Jennifer Bailey walked up the middle aisle, Harold a couple of steps behind her. She walked slowly, but purposefully, with perfect posture.

Shanahan wondered what she thought, seeing the mammoth crowd for her sister, who had in many ways played second to Jennifer, the successful attorney general of the state of Indiana, political power broker and often spokesperson for the city's black community. Was she getting a preview of her own send-off? Or was she surprised her sister had gathered so many followers?

Coming in to take her hand was the US congressman from the Seventh District. Shanahan looked at the program he was handed when they entered. The congressman was scheduled to speak. So was a deputy mayor. So were several others. It would be a long afternoon that would end only after the long ride out to Crown Hill Cemetery for the graveside service and burial.

Maureen, at Shanahan's suggestion, took the empty seat next to Mrs Tice. Shanahan made his way to Mrs Thompkins, who seemed to be

101

disengaging from her conversation with fellow commission member, Daniel Holcomb.

'Hard at work?' he asked her.

It took her a moment to place him. She smiled. 'That's cold. The truth is yes and no. I'm not trying to sell houses, but it's important. If I run for citywide office,' she said.

'Mayor, for example.'

'Yes. I need to show support for this community and for social services. I might not get much of a percentage as a Republican here, but I can't win without some support.'

'I might vote for you just for being honest about your motives. Who was closer to Alexandra Fournier, you or Holcomb?'

'Politically they appear to be more aligned, but I don't think they liked each other. She thought he spent money frivolously.'

'You'd think he'd want her backing.'

'She was pretty independent.'

'The Leonard Card thing. They disagree on that?'

'I'm getting the third degree here.' She smiled. 'Aren't I?'

'That's what I do. You think he would vote to let Card skate?'

'The conversation seemed to drift that way. For a liberal, Holcomb seemed a little soft on bad police behavior.'

'You?'

'Not so much. I'm law and order, no question, but the law applies across the board.'

'I'm impressed.'

'We may have different views on taxes, but

crime? That's where Mrs Fournier and I agreed. We got along.'

'So you might come down against Card?'

'I don't know. As it stands now – and this is confidential – there's not enough evidence against him. There's no question he was put in a dangerous situation. Collateral damage. Innocent people get caught up. The whole question of whether he was a decent kid not involved in gang activity might not matter. If the young man was there, why? And if he was killed by a bullet not intended for him, it would still be hard to punish Card under those circumstances.'

'Did Mrs Fournier have political ambitions?'

'I don't think so. She wanted to find homes and shape the lives of those who hadn't gotten a fair shake. She also didn't hold politicians in high regard. She never said so directly, but I think she believed her sister had to sell a bit of her soul. Mrs Fournier was a lovely woman, but a little naive. You don't get through life with a spotless soul.'

Sixteen

The lights in the vast auditorium blinked. People headed to the pews. The program was about to begin. The place went from quiet and sedate to loud and swinging. The sound of the choir filled the large space with ease. Perhaps Shanahan would have stayed awake if it weren't for the parade of speakers that followed the choir. Despite or because of the poetic rhythm of the oratory, for Shanahan, the sound turned into an unintelligible drone.

Even when his brain wasn't struggling against the swelling and inflammation, long, quivering quotes from the Scriptures sent him into dull gray emptiness. The words ceased to have meaning. 'The Lord has taken you from one path in order to pursue another . . .' Images crept in, faces of his parents, his brother. 'We have been blessed by your presence in a world that can be callous and uncaring.' His wife, the mother of his son, who left him so many years ago, visited him. Just a glance. It didn't trouble him. He had made peace with that part of his life. 'You have not only witnessed injustice, you've tried to right it, put lost souls back on the path of righteousness . . .' The kid, the dead face he saw in the window of Fournier's office appeared, pleading. For what? Shanahan could hear himself moan. Something shook him.

'Like Christ she could not leave the poor and the struggling by the road . . .'

He went somewhere. He didn't know the place. Or how long he was there. He heard a voice. A familiar and welcomed voice.

It was Maureen. She urged him to follow her. She was trying to help him up. A crowd had gathered around him, yet the pew had been cleared. Harold was there to steady Shanahan, who was unsteady at first. He gained strength and determination as he approached the end of the pew and more strength as they approached the exit.

'You've had a small seizure,' she told him.

'Is he going to be OK?' Harold asked.

Maureen nodded, retrieved a small pillbox from Shanahan's suit pocket, plucked a couple of pills. Shanahan swallowed.

'I have some water in my car,' Harold said as Shanahan slumped in the front seat of Maureen's car.

'I caused a scene,' Shanahan said, realizing with embarrassment that he had lost control of his bladder.

'It's a big place. It was like a Cubs' fan fell down in the bleachers in left field. The game continued,' Maureen said. 'Nobody noticed.'

'Who won?' Shanahan asked.

'The angels, I suspect. Home field advantage.'

Shanahan could hear the echoed sound of the speaker from the parking lot. Harold jogged to the Lexus and jogged back.

'Showoff,' Shanahan said to Harold when he returned.

Harold smiled.

'You better get back to Miss Bailey,' Shanahan said. 'She won't be happy as it is.'

'She sent me over,' Harold said. 'She wanted me to make sure you were all right.'

'I am.'

'She said she'd call you tomorrow,' Harold said.

He might have slept. Shanahan wasn't sure. He didn't know how much time had gone by before the car moved and he reengaged with day-to-day reality.

People began leaving the church. Small groups turned into larger ones, spilling out into the parking lot. The ritual was respected and Mrs Fournier was sent off.

Shanahan was quiet, tired and embarrassed. He said nothing on the drive home. The day had been a bust and it wasn't like he could do it over. He sat in the chair by the window.

Death had come suddenly, decisively for Alexandra Fournier. But that's not the usual way, he thought. For most it came in tiny steps, sometimes barely noticeable. Shanahan felt he'd had a tiny death today. Yes, yes, he chided himself. Death always comes suddenly. You are and then suddenly you aren't. And – he could feel the anger rising – why dwell on it? You big baby! He cursed himself. He almost said it out loud.

'I've been thinking,' Maureen said. 'I think I'm going to work from home for the next couple of days.'

The anger returned.

'Nothing going on in the office, and it's more comfortable here,' she said.

'I don't need a nurse,' he said, more harshly than he intended.

'This isn't just about you.'

'That's precisely why I don't want to be the focus.'

'The reason you had a seizure, *Mister* Shanahan, is that you didn't take your pills. They were on the shelf in the bathroom.' She sat on the arm of the sofa across from him. 'By the way, Mrs Tice said something interesting to me. It didn't register right away. Then the program started and I forgot about it. It's nothing, maybe.'

Shanahan was about to bet on nothing.

'She said "boys." Boys, plural.'

'What do you mean?'

I told her how hard it must be for her to go through all this tragedy. Mrs Fournier and the boy.'

'"The young are the most tragic," she said. "My heart broke when I learned about the boys."'

Shanahan sat up straight. No one mentioned two boys had died. True as it was, why wouldn't they?

He thought he might know. In fact, it seemed obvious now that he thought about it. He got up, found the phone and his notebook. He punched in the number for Mrs Tice.

'This is Shanahan. You have a moment?'

'Are you all right?' she asked.

'I'm fine. You told Maureen that it was a tragedy about the boys. More than one boy.'

'Yes. Nicky Hernandez and Justice King.'

Hernandez was the young man cleaning the gutters. Justice King?'

'Justice was accidentally shot by the police some time ago.'

'Was the cop Leonard Card?'

'I don't know. I just know it probably wasn't supposed to happen.'

'The boys? They both had connections with the center?'

'They were both aging out at about the same time. They were out on their own. I thought they'd make it.'

'So they knew each other?'

'They were close.'

'You didn't mention it before.'

'You didn't ask about it,' she said. 'Is there a connection?'

'Did the police talk to you or anyone about the boys knowing each other?'

'No.'

He understood. Black and Hispanic kids without family, but with juvy records, out on the street get killed. Happens all the time.

'Did Mrs Fournier talk about this Justice kid?'

'She was furious. She wouldn't talk about it, but when I brought it up she froze in anger in that way she did. We didn't have to talk. I knew that once someone made it on the outside that was her payment. That gave her what she needed to stay alive.

Shanahan called Collins. 'I know it's asking a lot, but I need to see the files on Justice King and Leonard Card.'

108

'The files? I don't have those. Internal Affairs has them.'

'Card's victim, Justice King, and Nicky Hernandez knew each other. Good friends.'

'Same gang, maybe.' It was a comment meant to throw cold water on the implications suggested by Shanahan's questions.

'You circling the wagons, Officer?'

'You're forgetting some things. Card couldn't hit the side of a barn with a brick at three feet, and at the time Mrs Fournier was about to ring your bell, Card was having a colonoscopy. I can get you the video if you want it.'

'You ever talk to Justice King's friends?'

'I didn't, no,' Collins said. 'Others might have.'

'I need to see the file on Card. I need to see what the oversight committee saw or sees, for that matter.'

'I'd like a harem, Shanahan.'

'I asked first.'

'You're not going to get it from me.'

'What happened to your suggestion of cooperation?'

'I don't have access to it. I've told you.'

'Maybe a reporter could stir things up. With Charles biting the dust and the connection between the two kids . . .'

'Don't threaten.'

'I'm sorry.'

'When was the last time you said you were sorry?' Collins asked.

'When John McCain was president.'

'McCain was never president. Oh, I see. I appreciate it even more.'

'Don't mention it,' Shanahan said.

'No, I mean it. I appreciate it.'

'No, I mean it. Don't mention it.'

Collins laughed. 'Give me a day to see what I can do.'

Seventeen

The blurry numbers on the clock radio gave him the only information readily available in the darkness: 11:53 p.m.

Maureen's moan wasn't about pleasure or pain, but a complaint about being taken from her sleep by the pounding on the door.

'Stay here,' Shanahan said. He felt his way to the bureau where he slid his fingers around the cool metal of the .45, slipping it from beneath the underwear in the top drawer. He knew the house by heart, even the creaks in the wood floor, which he could mostly dodge. A knock on the front door could mean someone else was already inside through the backdoor or a window.

The front porch light, switched on by a movement sensor, revealed the slightly pudgy, mostly tired face of Lieutenant Swann.

'Collins said I should come talk to you.'

Shanahan stifled the word 'now?' and stepped aside.

'Sorry about the hour,' Swann said. He came in, stood still, until Shanahan switched on a light in the living room.

Not even a moment after they had settled into the barely lit living room, Maureen appeared. She stood in the doorway, robe closed at the neck.

111

'May I get you some coffee, Lieutenant?'

'Did anyone ever tell you old people went to bed early?' Shanahan asked.

'She isn't old,' Swann said by way of defense.

'Can I whip you up some tiramisu or maybe banana flambé?' Shanahan said.

'No, thank you,' Swann said with a sad, appreciative grin. One could barely hear him. His head was buried in his hands.

'Coffee would take just a minute. Or there's whiskey,' she said. 'It's cold out.'

Shanahan nodded. 'Whiskies.'

'Collins said you wanted the file on Card,' Swann said.

'I was expecting something in a manila folder.'

'I'm the manila folder,' Swann said. He took the glass from Maureen. 'Thank you. I think this will help.'

Maureen gave the other glass to Shanahan. 'I'm climbing back in bed and see if I can't find that handsome young man in the forest.'

Shanahan handed her the .45. 'Put that in the silverware drawer.'

'Helluva way to mash potatoes,' she said as she disappeared into the hallway.

'Why did Collins send you?'

'I'm kind of the problem.'

'How's that?' Shanahan asked.

'The oversight committee was about to end the investigation into Card. There was a witness, but the witness wasn't sure he would testify. Mrs Fournier was furious. She wanted the name of the witness. Internal Affairs didn't have the name. Only an anonymous note. Fournier came to me for help.'

'Why did she come to you?' Shanahan sipped his whiskey.

'Same reason she was coming to you. Jennifer Bailey recommended me. If you remember, you and I worked on Bailey's missing niece. What was her name?'

'Jasmine,' Shanahan remembered. He'd seen her at the funeral.

'Jasmine. Anyway, Mrs Fournier didn't know where to go and she didn't know who to trust. Her sister recommended me.'

'But you're the problem, you said. I'm puzzled.'

'I am. I'm the reluctant witness,' Swann said.

'Jesus.' Shanahan understood. Swann was the witness Fournier wanted Swann to find. Swann's by-the-book reputation, the basis for his highly respected integrity and his slow but steady success, ran head on into the thin blue line of brother-cop loyalty.

'How about that? I'm the one who can ruin Card's career. His life.'

'Collins knows.'

'That's why, in his sardonic way, he put me on the case and why he's riding it so close.' Swann took a sip and put the glass on the table. 'I guess we were putting on the great stall, waiting for divine intervention or at least Lady Luck. Maybe Card would retire or kill himself. Fournier got tired of waiting and came to you.'

'Also on Bailey's recommendation,' Shanahan said. 'Bailey should have had a bigger Rolodex.'

113

Swann nodded.

'Card killed the kid on purpose?' Shanahan continued.

'Card had some other kid collared when Justice King came into the picture. The kid pulled out a cell phone. Card either mistook it for a weapon or he didn't care. He no doubt felt outnumbered. It was over in seconds. Nobody seemed to mind. But it turns out Justice was some sort of saint in the eyes of some and the story wasn't going to go away.'

'And you haven't made up your mind about what to say? How about just the truth as you saw it?'

'Simple, you think.'

'Not easy, but simple,' Shanahan said.

'I don't know what Card saw or thought he saw. I can say that a good cop, a good man with cop training wouldn't have shot that kid. And this isn't the first mistake Card made that ended in an unnecessary death. Also a black kid.'

There was a long silence.

'A couple of days and the committee decides based on the facts they have,' Swann said.

'Two questions. Did Card know there was a witness? If so, how?'

'As I understand it, the committee knew the decision was on hold because there *might* be a witness. That was based on my anonymous note and that fact was probably conveyed through the lawyers. If there's no corroboration, he'll walk.'

'Could Card have suspected you?'

'He didn't know I was there. I was doing a little surveillance on a drive-by. Some of my gang-bangers were there. Everyone, and there were a dozen or more of them, scattered when Justice King went down. I waited a few seconds, drove up and told him I just rolled in. It's in my hands. Do I let the clock run out?'

'You've decided.'

'I have?'

'You told me. I work for Bailey.'

Swann picked up his glass. There was a gulp left. He took it.

'You knew that.'

Swann nodded. 'I needed a nudge.'

'But you're not happy about it.'

'No,' Swann said. 'From the beginning, there was no good end.'

'Who needs Socrates?'

'How are you feeling?' Jennifer Bailey asked. Shanahan put the phone on speaker and set it on the counter. He only had use of one hand, so holding a phone and doing anything else was impossible. He dropped two slices of cinnamon bread in the toaster.

'Good. I missed my morning pills yesterday.'

'One of the many hazards of old age,' she said.

'And a diminished brain.'

'The subject of my call.'

'Let me give you a report before you show me the door.'

Maureen came shuffling in, slippers half on. 'Your sister knew the boy Card killed,' Shanahan continued. 'She was also aware there was a witness to the killing of young Justice King, but not who or whether the witness would testify. I

115

think that's why she came to me. I can't know that for sure. She was making a lot of noise because without an eyewitness Officer Leonard Card would skate.'

Maureen poured herself a cup of coffee and sat at the table to listen.

'She hammered the police first. I know that. And not getting a satisfactory response she came to me.'

'Are you telling me that this policeman Card killed off my family to keep his pension?'

'It's a valid if not compelling motive. But there are significant problems with it. Card didn't have the skill to kill Alexandra or Charles the way they were killed. He had an alibi for Alexandra and I'm betting he had one for Charles.'

'He could have hired it done?'

'Collins ran his financials. He was in debt, but not in a desperate way. A mortgage on his house. A loan on his car. The question really is why would he care if Charles lived or died even if he could afford a professional hitman? Charles was behind bars in Michigan City when Card killed the kid. And, I'm sorry, but Charles didn't seem like the kind of guy who cared whether some kid got whacked. What would he have to do with it?'

'I don't know,' she said.

'You've told me everything you know, right?'

'Yes,' she said. 'Do you believe it is worthwhile to continue?'

'Yes, but that's your call.' Shanahan waited out the silence.

'It is. Are you capable? You can do this?'

116

'I will be doing this, Miss Bailey. The only question is whether I do that for you or my other client.'

'Nicky Hernandez,' she said.

'Yes.'

'I thought so. I need Harold today. Do what you can, however you can. Get well. He'll be available tomorrow at noon. Who is this witness, Mr Shanahan?'

'Lieutenant Swann.'

'Good God,' she said. 'This means . . .'

'You tell no one until the time is right.'

'You're asking me . . .'

'No, telling you. Lives and careers are on the line. And there's something else going on, something bigger than a rogue cop. I don't want to blow it now.'

The toast popped up. Shanahan jumped.

Maureen laughed. 'Tough guy,' she said.

Maureen meant what she said about staying home. Shanahan used the noon sun, as warm as it was going to get, to rake the leaves. He was able to use his body and right arm to guide the rake. It was awkward, but doable. Maureen bagged the leaves. The fresh, cool air felt good. The trees on the neighboring lawns and in the stretch of land along the creek below still held some red and gold patches, striking, even without sunlight, against a sky of gray and silver. When winter fully arrived, and that would be soon, there would only be shades of gray. The notion that a sniper had a clear shot at them if he was so inclined wasn't lost on Shanahan. But the sniper had a clear shot at him on the day Alexandra was killed and didn't take it.

To Shanahan, this reinforced the notion of a hired killer. The client only paid for one killing. It would be like buying a Cadillac and the salesman throwing in a Chevrolet because it was there.

Still, it didn't add up. Fournier only knew there was a witness. She didn't have the only vote on Card. Why would Card up the ante by killing her? He wasn't the brightest bulb on the tree, but he was a cop with some savvy. And Charles? What did he have to do with anything other than this mystery company called Tyrus? No connections between Tyrus and Card could be made. Yet Charles was iced professionally. And poor Nicky Hernandez. His connection seemed obvious. He could identify the intruder. He was an accidental witness much like his friend, Justice King.

Shanahan heard his name, the sound broken by a gust of wind that scattered the leaves. He had a sense they were escaping during a temporary dereliction of duty. He didn't know where his mind had been. He hadn't seen Maureen go.

But she stood in the doorway, phone in hand, auburn hair tousled by the wind, looking like autumn herself.

The call was from Collins.

'Card had an iron-clad alibi when Charles was shot. A young masseuse in Noblesville. Make that a barely-clad alibi.'

'But it works.'

'It's on tape too, if we want it. Parking lot. Going in, coming out. Time-stamped.'

'Too good. His alibis are too good.' Shanahan thought for a moment. 'Her name wasn't Samantha, was it?'

'Pearl, I think. Asian. Who's Samantha?'

'Probably nobody. A car in his driveway. Ran the plates. Drew a blank.'

'Swann is writing up his report on the Justice King death,' Collins said.

'Good.'

'Might make Card more talkative,' Collins said.

'You going to talk to him?'

'That would make things official and we would get all caught up in Internal Affairs.'

'You want me . . .'

'I'm not asking for anything. Just thinking out loud,' Collins said.

'Tell Swann to turn his report in tomorrow afternoon. That will give me tomorrow to shake Card's cage.'

Shanahan often drifted off during the day, but he was not so blessed at night. Instead, he was haunted by a kind of cosmic loneliness, which, if allowed, would inhibit his breathing. It helped to walk, even through the empty rooms. Sometimes he would sit in his chair. If he couldn't shake it, he would step outside. The fresh, cold air in his lungs helped dispel the feeling of suffocating.

The fact that Card had two perfect alibis was damning, but not proof of his innocence,

Shanahan thought. But while Shanahan could grasp a reason for the cop to want Alexandra dead because of her position on Card's so-called 'accidental' shooting, the sleepless detective couldn't rationalize why Card would need Charles to suffer the same fate. Charles was locked away in Michigan City when the first kid went down. He had made that point to Jennifer Bailey as well. If they were professional hits, how did Card pay for them? One might be able to hire some local thug to off someone on the cheap, but these kinds of clean hits don't come cheap. It occurred to Shanahan as he meandered about in the dark that the deaths of Justice King and Nicky Hernandez were connected to each other but not necessarily to Alexandra and Charles. Nicky and Justice were not killed by a sniper or at least not using the sniper's MO. Was there a connection beyond their friendship and temporary home at Second Chance? There was a connection between Alexandra and her brother: Tyrus Investments. Whatever those investments were, it appeared Charles sweet-talked Alexandra out of them.

He was eager for morning to come.

Shanahan stood at the front window, waiting for Harold. Maureen was gone. She was inspecting a house on the northeast side. Collins called earlier to share some information. In Charles's wallet, they found three bank deposit receipts, each for $9,000, and each from a different major bank. It was clear that he was avoiding the IRS requirement that financial institutions have to report deposits over a certain amount. The fact that they were made at major banks suggested Charles wanted the maximum in geographic mobility and as much anonymity as was possible these days. The deposit, Collins said, sounding defeated, was a cash transaction, which eliminated the ability to trace the source of the funds. While the way all this was handled didn't require a financial genius, it did show some sophistication in that regard as well as a criminally devious mind. Had they been able to trace the funds, Shanahan was sure it would lead to Tyrus Investments, whoever the hell they were.

The Lexus pulled into the driveway at noon.

'Are we gonna just sit here?' Harold asked.

'I don't know.' Leonard Card was what was left. His dirty Jeep Cherokee was in the drive. He was likely home. If he didn't provide the next step, Shanahan might as well toss it in. Nobody alive, except Leonard Card, could be linked to the boys' deaths or the demise of the two elder siblings. It didn't look good. Surely, a slack-jawed bully, a loser like Leonard wasn't Tyrus.

'You going in?'

'I suspect so. You have a date?'

'Good thing I don't.'

'This is the only place I know to go, the only person to talk to. I don't know what to say or do.'

'You don't have a plan?' Harold pulled the ear bud from his ear.

'Right, but I often don't have a plan. There's something here I'm not seeing.'

Shanahan started to get out, but decided to tell Harold a story.

'One of the tests I had was from an ophthalmologist after I explained that if I put something down on my left I couldn't find it. They gave me a visual field test and discovered that I was blind here and there after the second operation. The inflammation and swelling inhibited the gathering of visual information or the processing of it. Apparently it's not like being in the dark or there is a dark place here and there. My mind fills it in somehow, and it all looks perfectly normal, but like magic, the rabbit is gone. I'm missing something that others see. A pen, a glass, perhaps a human.'

'I don't think you are the only one missing something,' Harold said. He laughed.

'Who else?'

'Everybody. Mrs Fournier didn't know. The police don't know. Seems to me different people have different pieces the others don't see. But things are done. People die. Money changes hands. Pieces are being moved.'

'And?'

'Maybe instead of finding out what people know, we find out what or who they don't know,' Harold said. He leaned forward. 'Keep the car parked here. I want to make sure he sees you. Made him nervous the last time.'

'I like making people nervous.'

Shanahan got out of the car, headed up Leonard Card's driveway.

*   *   *

Card looked particularly grizzled. Shanahan realized why.

'Haven't seen your girlfriend in a while?' he asked the unhappy cop at the door.

'Girlfriend?'

'Last time I was here. Silver Malibu.'

'Somebody paying you to keep track of my life?'

'Yeah, the world is a funny place, isn't it?'

'Well, I believe you are trespassing.'

'I have some news for you,' Shanahan said.

'Spill it.'

'How about you invite me in?'

'How about I break every bone in your face?'

'You really think that beating up a senior citizen will help your case in front of the review board?'

'Just make me feel better.'

'Then I wouldn't be able to fill you in on the development in your hearing. It's not going to go the way you think it is.'

Card was quiet.

'And there is a witness sitting out there in the Lexus. You don't like having witnesses around, I'm told.'

'Come in.'

The living room looked like it was once the normal living area for a modest two-bedroom home. A substantial couch, pillows now stained and askew. Two flower-patterned upholstered chairs. Space had been cleared, though awkwardly, for a giant-screen TV, which blocked the front picture window. At one end of the room, more space had been cleared for weight-lifting. Aesthetics played no part in the

123

decisions. Obviously, priorities had changed. It was a man cave.

'We got a talk 'n go situation here,' Card said, his face inches from Shanahan's. It was an intimidation technique used by cops and the gang members who emulated them. His eyes were old and evil, dissipated by years of unhealthy habits and bad attitude. Yet his body was tightly muscled, like a pit bull. Even at his fittest, Shanahan thought, he wouldn't have wanted to come up against Card, who was, by age at least, ten years beyond his prime.

'Been divorced two, maybe three years?' Shanahan asked.

'Don't make yourself comfortable.' He rubbed the stubble on his cheeks.

'There is a witness to the killing of Justice King. And the witness said you killed the boy without cause.'

'Is that it?' Card grinned. 'The dead are usually a quiet lot.'

'That smile explains everything,' Shanahan said. It explained the sad death of Nicky Hernandez. Shanahan would let the police drive that truth into Card's heart. He felt his work was done. He moved toward the door. He would have liked to ask to use the bathroom to check out drug use or other health problems, as well as evidence of someone staying with him. But even a dumb cop like Card knew that trick.

'You come all the way over here to tell me that? Nothing better to do? You might want to retire,' the cop said, still smirking, as the clean, chilly air greeted Shanahan's escape from the

124

stale environs of Card's retreat. 'You are way behind the curve,' Card shouted after him.

'How'd it go?' Harold asked.

'Magic,' Shanahan said. 'Like you said, he revealed what he didn't know. He killed Hernandez because he thought Hernandez was the secret witness.'

Eighteen

Shanahan and Collins met near the Museum of Contemporary Art and walked down to the canal.

'You don't like your office?' Shanahan asked. He liked the idea of being outside, but didn't look forward to walking back up the hill.

'Not a desk jockey at heart. What's up?'

'What kind of history does Card have?'

'What do you mean?'

'Homicide? Vice? What?'

'I'll double-check, but Homicide. No, I think Vice and now Gangs.'

'I think you need to get Card's alibi for the morning the Hernandez kid was killed.'

'Even though he's got two solid ones for the others?'

'Yes.'

'Nobody has an alibi for five a.m. No one is up that early unless they're making donuts.'

'It will give him something to think about,' Shanahan said. 'There's no real evidence that the same killer did all three.'

'In fact . . .'

'In fact, the MO was different. And we all assumed the kid was murdered because he saw the killer tossing Fournier's office and could identify him. That was a presumption.'

Collins gave Shanahan a sharp look. 'A pretty fucking logical presumption.'

'That's what a cop would think and what a cop would do,' Shanahan said. 'The office could have been messed up after the boy was killed to connect the boy's death with that of Mrs Fournier's. Link the deaths you link the alibis. If Card had a solid alibi for one murder he might be able to parlay that into two.'

'Why the kid? And who knew he was going to be there at that hour, on that day?' Collins asked.

'Card heard there was going to be a witness, thanks to Swann's anonymous note. Card didn't know who until he found out, as I did later, that both King and Hernandez had lived at Second Chance and that they were good friends. Since Swann initially covered his steps, Card assumed it was Hernandez, King's best friend, who was going to testify. Card thinks this whole witness thing is old news since Hernandez was eliminated.'

'And you're saying Card knew exactly when Hernandez was going to be in Fournier's backyard?'

'Fournier was a creature of habit. The boy was there every Wednesday morning at that time. With a little bit of surveillance, it wouldn't have been hard for Card to figure that out. He had all the time in the world. And there was an undercover car hanging around the community center. There's probably a dozen kids willing to testify to that. Card knew Mrs Fournier's standard routine.'

Collins kicked at the pebbles on the path. 'What you're saying here is that these deaths aren't connected after all.'

'*Maybe* that's what I'm saying.'

127

'That *is* what you're saying. And you're saying that all this work to figure out the murder of Mrs Fournier, subject of serious media attention, has been for naught, while we may have closed an internal affairs case no one particularly cares about.'

Shanahan said nothing right away as Collins paced by the slow-moving muddy water.

'Two kids are dead.'

'All right. I'm not the most sensitive guy on the block. But you get my gist. And that goes for you too. Right. You're getting paid to find the murderer of Jennifer Bailey's sister.'

'Collins?'

'What?'

'If I'm right, the guy who killed Hernandez had to know Fournier was going to get it and when.'

'Officer Perfect Alibi.' Collins shook his head. 'Maybe we haven't wasted our time.'

'Well, that's a thought, isn't it?'

'So is Collins happy or unhappy?' Maureen asked, taking a corner off a slice of pizza.

'Mostly unhappy. The media and the mayor are impatient.'

'You?' She took a sip of a glass of Chilean wine. The news, coming from the small TV set on the kitchen counter six feet away, seemed to underline Shanahan's comments about the pressure to come up with something on the deaths of Alexandra Fournier and her brother, Charles Bailey. Collins's name was also bandied about.

'Me? Nobody knows my name.'

'Hurt your feelings?'

'A blessing,' he said.

'You're making progress and so is Collins.'

'Seems so. Fortunately we were able to nail down some facts that were previously allusive and sent us in the wrong direction. We still have no direction. What we do have is the probability that Card had some foreknowledge of Alexandra and her brother's deaths. And the fact that the only assets that could have enabled Charles to make such significant cash deposits was his connection to Tyrus Investments, whatever or whoever they are.'

'The other thing that Charles had was a map,' Maureen said.

'Yes.'

'Real estate.' She plucked another slice of pizza from the box, put it on Shanahan's plate, followed by some lightly dressed romaine. 'You have to have your greens.'

'Isn't there some parsley on the pizza?'

'A sprinkle or two.'

'I rest my case,' Shanahan said.

'The police remain silent on the murder of Alexandra Fournier and her brother, Charles Bailey,' said the female news anchor in the background as the colorful lights of the TV bounced around on the walls. 'However, a spokesman verified what we reported earlier. Both deaths came from a sharpshooter at a distance, fueling rumors that they were professional hits.'

'Someone let that out,' Shanahan said. He was surprised.

'We'll have more from weapons experts

commenting on that, Denise,' interrupted a male voice, 'tonight at eleven. And we'll be asking a former district attorney why it's taking so long to get a lead on these brazen daylight murders.'

'How about a dog?' Shanahan asked. He knew the question would seem to come out of nowhere. There was a moment of silence.

'No, thanks – the pizza is filling.'

'But you can't walk a pizza.'

'What brought that up?'

'Wandering the halls at night. A little life in the place might be good.'

'What am I? Chopped liver?' she asked.

'That time of night you're in France or someplace snoring through a plate of *manicotti*.'

'That would be Italy.'

'I rest my case again.'

'I don't need a shih-tzu yipping at my heels all day long.'

'I was thinking more like a Belgian Shepherd.'

'Oh,' she said.

'Ex-police or military dog. Well-behaved. Mature.'

'Kind of like a canine version of you.'

'Maybe a little younger.'

They watched the *Kennel Club Murder Case*. It seemed fitting, considering a night of conversation about murder and dogs. Maureen put the film on pause when the phone rang.

'I have some information,' said Collins in a slightly muffled tone.

'You're working late. That's not like you.'

'Desperate times call for desperate measures. And it's important.'

'And you called me?'

'It was either you or Batman, but the spotlight blew a fuse. As I expected, Leonard Card's alibi for the early morning Nicky was killed was as we expected. At five a.m., he was asleep in his own bed at his own home, alone. It may or may not be true, but it is believable. What's interesting is that Card has used the police department as a billiard table. Not Homicide. Yet. But everything else. Vice, Gangs, where he was up to a few weeks ago and before that, Organized Crime.'

'Organized Crime?' Shanahan asked.

'I thought you'd pick up on that.'

'You can meet some interesting people in Organized Crime. Contract killers, for example.'

'I'll do what I can to find out who.'

Shanahan put on his brown tweed sport coat, and a pressed blue button-down, straight from the dry cleaners' plastic wrap.

'We're meeting downtown,' Shanahan said in defense of Maureen's mock-jealous, accusatory look.

'All this for Mrs Thompkins? You have a thing for real estate agents?' Maureen asked.

'I do.'

She handed him the map she had printed out of the Eastside. She highlighted the areas that had been highlighted on Charles's map. He kissed her on the cheek.

'Saving the passion and the fashion for your girlfriend, I see.'

'Patachou on the Park. All of those professionals. I didn't want to embarrass her.'

'You look great. Patachou and Thompkins don't deserve you.'

Patachou was popular, clean, modern, and somewhat cold. The front opened to a city street and the back to a garden, set in the state government area of downtown. The grand, ornate, domed Capitol was a short walk as were blocks of monumental-looking government offices stretching across the end of the canal.

Shanahan was amused that his arrival was greeted with stares. Despite his age and attire, the idea of getting out of the back seat of a car with a driver caused a minor stir.

Contrary to what he expected, his date was not fashionably late. She was at the table with a cup of coffee and orange juice. Thompkins was a woman devoted to primary colors. Today she wore a blue dress that could not be any bluer. With her whitish, goldish hair and intensely red lips, her very existence spoke of patriotism as theater.

'Thank you for meeting me downtown. You've saved me a couple of hours.'

Shanahan had looked at her politically oriented website and, while he was not fond of her views of how the world should work, he liked her. How much of what she said, she actually believed, he was unsure. To fit into the current conservative club she carefully groomed, curated her image as a tough, take-no-prisoners fiscal Grinch, don't-tread-on-me militant and ultra traditionalist when it came to social issues. But unlike many members of her party she couldn't bring herself to say the earth was only 5,000 years old.

'You have some downtown properties?' Shanahan asked after their order was taken.

'Oh, yes, lofts in converted factories and old apartment buildings are booming. The closer to downtown the better. Record sales, record prices.'

'I had no idea.' He didn't. Maureen's sales and listings were pretty middle-market.

'I have a nice little residence right in the heart of the city for five.'

'Five what?'

She smiled. 'No kidding. You didn't want to meet with me for real estate advice. Now, I'm not complaining, but why are we here?'

'Real estate advice? Yes. Some. I have some questions. But I'm also curious about why you agreed to meet with me. I don't begin to qualify for one of your mortgages. I can't help you politically and frankly, I wouldn't.'

'Why I agreed to meet is simple. I try very hard, very hard to never say "no." I am also on the police oversight board, as you know, and being on the right side of the disposition of the case you're working on is important to me and to my ambition. I promised you I'd help if I could.'

'How does it work, this committee?'

'We read transcripts of interviews, look at personnel files, performance reviews, arrest reports, personnel evaluations, hear witnesses.'

'Would you talk to the subject? In this case, Leonard Card?'

'Yes. He presented himself to the commission.'

'What did you think?'

'It's probably not wise of me to go much further. Suffice it to say, I wouldn't want him to marry my sister.'

'Did you meet with him privately?'

'For an hour.'

'Did anyone else on the committee?'

'We all had that option.'

'Do the files contain personal information? If someone wanted to contact him, they could, couldn't they?'

'I believe so,' she said.

'Here's a map,' Shanahan said as the server arrived.

She took the map as a colorful plate of fresh fruit and yogurt was set out before her.

'What am I looking at?' She waved the paper as if it had come from the gutter.

'I was hoping you could make sense of it.' He looked down as his BLT made with mozzarella slid in front of him. Life was good, he thought.

'From my perspective, it takes the lively, rejuvenated area of the city and extends its influence into nearby, currently impoverished areas. It could be someone's idea of the direction of the city's redevelopment.'

'Is it realistic?'

'It's not done with any graphic expertise, therefore I doubt if any of it is from a professional.'

'Forget the quality for the moment. Does the concept make sense?'

'There are two problems, at least. Even though

the city is doing well, development has always dilly-dallied behind plans and certainly expectations. I would put my money behind Fountain Square and Fletcher Place if I were younger and expected to live long enough to collect.' She dipped a strawberry into the yogurt and took a bite.

'This,' she said, handing back the map, 'seems quite ambitious. It would demand tons of money and city population growth I certainly don't see happening in my lifetime. Where did you get this?'

'Off the body of Charles Bailey, more or less. Later, we found significant money, at least significant for Charles, deposited in bank accounts with his name on it.'

She was quiet for a while. She took another bite, looked around, finally settling her eyes on his. 'Mr Shanahan, I sell expensive houses. Though I'm not immune to looking into the future, that's not my expertise. I'm not an investor or a developer. But what I'd say is that this map, if it's meant as development, is incredibly amateur in its ambition as well. But even if it were valid in terms of city planning, we would be talking about something that pays off way down the road. I can't imagine people getting killed over this map.' She shrugged, then seemed to change her mind. 'Who knows?' She shook her head. She looked at the map again. 'It is interesting. I just don't see that kind of thing happening, though there is a certain logic to it. It's forward thinking. No one that smart would render it so primitively.'

The quality of the map seemed to put her off more than what it was a map of.

Shanahan worried that the presentation was at fault. But he gave up. He didn't explain that this was a computer printed map from Google, enhanced by colored markers, recreating the pattern from Shanahan's hole-filled memory of Charles's unsteady interpretation of what he might have merely overheard.

But what made sense to him is that it would take too long for a project like this to pay off for most American investors, known for their impatience and their shirking of long-term planning. Who would undertake such a project? Someone young, ambitious, and at least somewhat optimistic. Holcomb popped into his head.

'Anymore news on Card?' he asked.

'That's one of the reasons I'm downtown. Meeting this afternoon. A witness has come forward. I thought you might have had something for me.'

Shanahan had to show some good faith. Giving up Lieutenant Swann a few minutes early would harm no one.

'A cop.'

'Really.'

'Lieutenant Swann saw the kid go down and after some soul-searching is willing to testify. Eyewitness. That party's over for Card. Do me a favor.'

'If I can.'

'Ask Card if he knows anything about a company called Tyrus.'

'You want to tell me?'

'I don't know. It's a stab in the dark. But if I were a little mouse in the room, I'd love to see Card's face when he sees Swann. I'd be watching not just Card's reaction but the committee members' as well.'

'Just when I think you've told me everything . . .'

'You might get a resolution on Justice King's death, but no other . . .'

'The case slipping away?'

'I'll tell you when I know. I promise, Tyrus means something. Just don't know what.'

Thompkins looked at him. She wanted more.

'I might be in a position to have the media come to you for comment when this shakes out,' Shanahan said. 'That is, if I get something out of this.'

She smiled again. It was so practiced it seemed natural.

Nineteen

Sometimes the only thing you can do is nothing. And nothing loomed big on Shanahan's afternoon. He called Jennifer Bailey, reported what he could with the explanation that he expected Card to go down on the killing of Justice King and that if that didn't create a big break in the other murders then he wasn't sure what would. He sent Harold back to Bailey.

His moment's rest in front of the window turned into two hours. He awoke surprisingly clearheaded when Maureen whooshed past him toward the bathroom.

'Get your coat,' she said. 'We have to go out and scrounge for dinner.'

That meant a trip to Marsh's, a nearby downtown supermarket.

'Therapy?' Shanahan suggested.

'If you know what's good for you . . .'

'I do. I do.' Five minutes in produce and she'd be a new woman, but the metamorphosis would have to wait. Shanahan found himself on the other end of a call from Mrs Thompkins.

'I have a little video for you to see,' she said, trying to explain how she could send it to his computer. Shanahan, realizing he was out of his depth after he heard the words 'formats,' 'megabytes,' and 'compressed,' called Maureen to the phone. Maureen was not just reluctant, she was peeved. She made angry faces while sounding civil, almost sweet. He went to the kitchen to fix her a drink.

The conversation not only turned out well – the two had agreed to meet for lunch at some unspecified place at some unspecified time.

'You guys got downright cozy,' Shanahan said of the flattery obviously going both directions between the two real estate agents.

'She's nice, but she's decided my name is "Maurie." I never liked that. Dad called me that when he wanted something. It was never good.'

Maureen was not fond of her father, but apparently she let it slide with her new friend. Shanahan thought there was a hierarchy among realtors as there was for doctors, lawyers and any other profession. Thompkins was a legend in that profession and a growing threat, as some saw it, as a city leader. There might have been a little, rare insecurity in Maureen's behavior, perhaps even a small lapse in sincerity.

'Some people like to put an "ie" or "y" after people's names. Johnny, Billie. They think it's friendlier,' Shanahan said.

'It trivializes them, makes them harmless,' Maureen said. 'What if I called you Shanahanie?'

'Makes me sound like the Irish-Hawaiian god I am.'

What the woman had was more serious. Thompkins had a video of the committee meeting. She was able to attach it to an email she sent to Maureen's computer. Judging by the quality of the sound, abrupt movement and poor framing, it was likely a surreptitious exercise, probably from an iPhone. There were moments when the images were blurred by fingers in front of the lens. Sometimes the movement was fast, awkward and askew, as if Thompkins had moved too quickly to catch something important. The sound was poor and at moments unintelligible. She was definitely doing this on the down low. Perhaps it wasn't all that risky, but it would be embarrassing if caught.

Maureen verified the secret nature of the video by repeating Thompkin's warning that this was for 'their eyes only.'

After Shanahan got over the idea of the secret taping and the nearly magical ability of sending it electronically within minutes of the event, he settled in to see what he could see.

The first transition was when Card came into the room. The screen showed five people in office attire seated at a round table. Shanahan recognized only Daniel Holcomb. Presumably Thompkins was behind the camera and was therefore out of the frame. Holcomb picked up his pen and noted something, but obviously not making eye contact with Card who seemed, in the next few moments, to glance at each of the attendees, except Holcomb.

A voice said: 'This is Officer Leonard Card, who has asked to be part of this hearing, especially in light of new information. As you all know we are not only behind schedule in rendering a determination and recommendation in this case, there has been increasing interest and we might say pressure to resolve this fairly but expeditiously.'

'Officer Card, we are about to do that,' Holcomb said, and still did not make eye contact with Card.

Shanahan was impressed with Holcomb's cool professionalism.

One of the women at the table stood, went to the door. She went out and came back in, followed by Lieutenant Swann.

'This is Lieutenant Swann from IMPD Homicide.'

Card's eyes closed for a full ten seconds. Holcomb tossed his pen onto the pad with what appeared to be, for a moment, restrained disgust. Unless one were specifically looking for such minor tells, it is not likely they'd be noticed. Too small and too quick. And people were still being seated. Shanahan had Maureen back up the action and asked to go through it again. Card's eyes closed and when he opened them he looked down at the tabletop. Card was surprised and upset. Holcomb was surprised and angry. Clearly, they were expecting someone, anyone, else.

'Lieutenant Swann,' Holcomb said, 'we were under the impression that the witness we were to hear from today was present at the scene of the incident at the time of the incident.'

'That is correct,' Swann said.

'I've gone through the arrest report and several witness reports and I don't recall coming across your name.'

Swann apologized and explained how he had come to witness the incident and why he had been reluctant to report it at the time.

'What changed your mind?' came the voice of Mrs Thompkins.

Holcomb clearly didn't like the interruption or what could be considered a challenge to his authority.

'The death of the victim's best friend, Nicky Hernandez,' Swann said, choking on his words. 'I should say murder of young Mr Hernandez. Too many young minority kids are written off as expendable.'

'Am I hearing you say that the unfortunate death of one youth has led you to change your testimony with regard to the unfortunate accident of another?'

'I have not changed my testimony. I have not testified until now.'

'That's not the fault of this committee. You have had every opportunity, not to mention duty, to step forward before now.' Holcomb was about to ask another question when Card stood. He did so with such force his chair tipped back, hitting the floor.

'You told me you got there after the gun went off!' Card yelled out angrily.

'Is that true, Lieutenant Swann?' Holcomb said. 'As I understand it, you were in the area doing some surveillance, just driving by . . .' He stopped suddenly. 'Marilyn, could you arrange some coffee for us. I think this may take . . .' He let the sentence drift off. 'So Lieutenant Swann, I stand corrected. You have not testified. But you have not mentioned that you witnessed the actual event until now. Late at the very least.'

'Can you go back again,' Shanahan asked, 'to the spot where Card screams and start again. Stop when Holcomb asks for coffee.'

142

They watched. Shanahan asked for a third viewing. 'What are you seeing?' Maureen asked.

'Holcomb making a huge mistake and recovering like the master attorney he is.'

'Tell me,' Maureen said.

'I read all the files the committee viewed. Swann wasn't even mentioned, let alone the fact that Swann had been doing a stakeout in the area. Other cops may have known he stopped by, but that wasn't in any of the interviews. This means that at some point between King's death and now, Holcomb and Card talked privately. Holcomb, among other things, seems to be acting as Card's secret defense attorney.'

Shanahan could imagine some intense discussions between the two: 'Tell me everything. Every detail, every second,' Holcomb would say. They might have discussed Swann's arrival, taken him for his word and determined he wouldn't be a factor. After all, Swann said he wouldn't be. Judging by the body language when Swann entered the committee room, he wasn't expected. Card and Holcomb no doubt thought the new, late witness was some gang-banger whose testimony they could easily impeach. Depending on what Holcomb knew, Card thought there would be no witness. Hernandez was dead.

'Why would Holcomb play that role?' Maureen asked.

'Answer that and we may have the keys to the kingdom.'

They watched the rest of the video. Holcomb had gathered his calm. Card said nothing. Swann, under Holcomb's smooth and seemingly unbiased questions, found his memories clouded and his observations muddied. In the end, Swann could not say he saw Card 'actually aim' the gun at King before he fired. Not one hundred percent sure.

Card would likely walk on this one and, if he did, it would be hard to connect him to Hernandez's death. Attempts would look like harassment.

Shanahan called a key reporter from one of the local TV stations and told her that the police review board had reached a decision on the troubled cop, Leonard Card, reminded her what it was about and that they had file footage on the case. He provided contact information for Mrs Thompkins. He called Thompkins.

'Spin it any way you want,' he told her. 'Holcomb would if he had the first opportunity.'

'Thanks. It's a shame how it turned out. Card's going to get out of this,' she said. 'I'm going to try to chain him to his desk. But for you, I wish I could have been more helpful. It's kind of like poker. Read 'em and weep.'

'I'm not weeping, Mrs Thompkins. Neither should you. In keeping with the tone, I'd suggest you keep your powder dry.'

'Look at you,' Maureen said. 'Giving each other tips on make-up.'

'How about some pumpkin ravioli?' Maureen asked as she parked her Toyota in the lot of Marsh's Supermarket. A cold, fine mist came down causing halos to form around the light poles. A couple of degrees colder, it would be light snow. The cold, the real cold was coming.

He buttoned the top button of his jacket and pulled down his stocking cap as far as he could and still see.

Maureen was inside before Shanahan got to the automatic door. So little exertion, yet he was exhausted.

The store was crowded. The human instinct as the weather changed was to get in provisions. Maureen moved through the crowds easily. Shanahan couldn't keep up. He waited by the door.

Twenty

Kowalski joined Maureen and Shanahan at the Slippery Noodle, a blues bar just south of downtown. Given the time of evening, Shanahan would have liked to have begged off, but Kowalski was eager to get together after hearing about Holcomb and the secret tapes. Meeting at the bar was Kowalski's idea because he had arranged to meet someone there later, quite likely a pretty woman whose day began after midnight.

Once past the hour and the volume, Shanahan relaxed a little. The club was old Indianapolis, nothing fancy. It had been around longer than he had, prospering despite the often-fickle public by always providing quality music.

Shanahan sat in the corner, listening to the band and sipping a whiskey. He would tell anyone who inquired that he felt like he'd been through the wringer, but wasn't sure anyone would know what that meant. Maureen was on her second rum and tonic when Kowalski showed up as happy as Gollum with the ring.

They moved away from the big room with the stage toward the bar, sacrificing the best in live blues for enough quiet to hear each other talk.

'If I look at your office, Kowalski, and I look at Holcomb's, I'd have some questions.'

'My clients are poorer. They steal a TV set or an iPhone,' Kowalski said. 'Holcomb's clients steal an old couple's retirement savings.'

'Still,' Shanahan said, 'he's pretty young . . .'

'And brash and showy.'

'So are you.'

'You have a point there, except for the young part. Are you trying to make me unhappy with my life? Money isn't everything.'

'No. But I'm betting being a criminal defense attorney isn't the only source of his income.'

'And somehow, some way, you think this is connected to our slippery cop.'

'And to land on Tenth Street, stretching down from Woodruff Place to Massachusetts Avenue.'

Maureen handed him a copy of the makeshift map.

'And to the deaths of Alexandra Fournier, her brother Charles, and Nicky Hernandez,' Shanahan added.

'On the other hand, Card is showing no signs of coming into some money?' Kowalski asked.

'No, but he may avoid losing his pension and staying out of prison – where cops typically don't do well – through Daniel Holcomb's legal counsel, not to mention his leadership on the board looking into his case.'

'What is Holcomb getting out of it is the question. May I keep the map?' Kowalski folded it and tucked it into his coat pocket.

'One other gaping mystery,' Shanahan said. 'The shooter.'

Kowalski leaned back. It was clear he was giving it some thought.

'Collins said that Card did a stint in the Organized Crime unit,' Shanahan said.

'That could tie the shooter to Card and explain what Card was doing for our rich criminal defense attorney. He thinks he's so good he can succeed in a life of crime.' Kowalski laughed.

'As an attorney, he stands the best chance,' Shanahan said.

'Maybe I can represent him.'

'Or get rid of Holcomb,' Maureen said, 'and you've eliminated the competition.'

'The criminally inclined global conglomerates won't be asking me to dinner, I guarantee you,' Kowalski said. 'And if they did, that's when I switch sides. Let me do some investigating on this property business. And Maureen, if you're able to find out who owns some of this land, let me know, especially those who own more than one parcel. Commercial and residential. We can make some calls, see if Daniel Holcomb rings a bell.'

'Or Tyrus Investments.'

'Somebody has to have signed something. There may be no official file but contracts, filed or not, have to have signatures.'

Shanahan shivered his way to Maureen's car while she held his arm and steadied his gait.

'I didn't mean to pull you so far into this,' Shanahan said to Maureen as they climbed into bed. 'You have your own work to do.'

'I'm enjoying myself,' she said. 'However, it will cost you.'

'How much?'

'Think restaurants. Think sauces and flaming desserts.'

'The stuff of nightmares.'

As habit was now demanding, Maureen drifted off to sleep quickly. Shanahan struggled. Morning meant a visit to the surgeon who, even though he'd doubled Shanahan's anti-seizure medication after the event in the church, said it was time for a check-up. The whole idea of seizures was bad enough. What was worse for Shanahan was the increased dependence upon Maureen. Other than a couple of bullets over seven decades, he was a healthy human specimen. He had always taken care of himself. And he would take care of her, he thought, not the other way around.

However, he believed he was now half a Shanahan physically – he was feeble and tired easily – and he was very unsure of the percentage of his wholeness he maintained mentally.

The exam was quick. He answered a few questions, did a few finger exercises, squeezed the doctor's hand and it was over. No change. Because of the seizures, the surgeon believed the inflammation and swelling remained. His left arm was nearly useless. More time, the doctor implied. Instead of gradually reducing the steroids, he was switched to a different type of steroid.

It was still morning. Outside was fresh, clear and cool. There would be sun today. Light but not heat. He wished he were recovering, but he'd have to be satisfied that things weren't getting worse. The case, on the other hand, was on the edge. It could go either way.

The days he would be on Jennifer Bailey's payroll were coming to an end, but in Shanahan's mind that didn't mean the investigation would. Necessarily. Shanahan had something to work with: the connection between Card and Holcomb. The video established the connection, but did not clarify it. Both people, who would not even know each other in the day-to-day world, except for their common interest in crime, had to be getting something from the connection.

'I have something to show you when we get home,' Maureen said.

'What?'

'I want to show you. Something I found while you were in the shower. I don't know if it means anything.'

'I almost didn't bring it up,' Maureen said, opening her laptop on the kitchen table as Shanahan unfolded the morning paper.

He heard the keyboard clicking away as he searched for news related to Fournier.

'Benzie's,' she said. The screen showed the image Shanahan had seen before when they were looking up Card's girlfriend, Samantha Byers.

'Yes?' Shanahan was puzzled. Nothing new. Samantha, probably a prostitute, had used the motel's address briefly as a mail drop.

Maureen moved the cursor to satellite view and clicked. From above Benzie's was a square box surrounded on all sides by a parking lot. The lot was large and could accommodate a few big rigs. At the back, the lot was bordered by mature bushes. There was a small gap in the wall of

150

shrubbery. Behind the lot and accessible through the gap was open field. On it was what appeared to be a house trailer.

'Have we found Samantha?' Shanahan said.

'What's this "we" stuff?' Maureen asked. 'And why so much stealth? If she were a prostitute and I were a John, I'd be a little wary of a hidden trailer.' She smiled in victory.

'What?' he asked.

'You remember the riddle that went around a few years ago? A father and son are in a car accident. The father dies instantly. The son is taken to the hospital. The doctor takes one look at him and says: "I can't operate on him! He's my son!" Since his father died in the accident, how can this be?'

'Because the doctor is the boy's mother. Yes, I remember. What does this . . .?'

'The shooter is a woman. Samantha Myers is the sniper, not a prostitute.'

Shanahan kissed her on the forehead.

'This is the Card–Holcomb connection. Card, through his work for the Organized Crime unit, got the hitman, or in this case, hitwoman, for Holcomb, who has probably never met Samantha or even knows her name.'

It made perfect sense. Holcomb, with his political ambition and his spotless family background, would keep the sleazy details at arm's length. The protection strategy comes from the mind of a lawyer or someone very, very clever.

'Now what? You'll call Captain Collins?'

'Just Collins. It'll take three hours to get to South Bend.'

'Why not just let the police do it all?'

'I want to make sure I'm right. And all they'll do is scare her away.'

He waved at Harold, who sat waiting patiently in the drive. Harold didn't wave back. Shanahan picked up the phone, called Collins. Got voicemail.

'Get to South Bend. It's a bit of a gamble, but there's a fifty-fifty chance I'll have the sniper for you, all tied up in a bow. I'll call you on your cell when it's time. Be ready to move quickly and with force. She's armed and dangerous. We'll likely be on the south side of South Bend.' Shanahan withheld all specifics.

Twenty-One

'Where to?' Harold asked.

'South Bend.'

Shanahan wasn't sure whether nothing flustered Harold or whether Harold was determined never to show surprise or frustration. He backed from the drive. Getting to Benzie's didn't require a map. Washington Street, the city's main east–west corridor, to Meridian Street, main north–south corridor. Turn right and keep driving for two and a half hours.

'Harold, could I get your opinion?' Shanahan asked when they finally escaped the outlying suburban remnants of the city and onto the flat, straight highway that cut through barren fields. Only months ago they gave up tons of corn and soybeans. 'Let's say you are God Almighty . . .'

'A minor leap of faith.'

'And you must punish three murderers. One found the person to do the killing. One paid the person to do the killing. And one who did the killing. Is any one of them guiltier than the other?'

'Hang all three of them.'

'All right, slightly different question. Two murderers this time. One murderer does it at a distance, coldly, quickly and possibly painlessly. The other does it up close and personal. The victim dies more slowly, scared and in serious pain.'

153

Harold shakes his head. 'Not my idea of fun, playing these games.'

'We're playing for real now.'

'We're going to see Samantha Byers,' Harold said.

'We are.'

'All this for a girlfriend?'

'Hired assassin. She's tried to stay off the grid, but maybe she's still clutching at the edge. I think she's more than a honey pot.'

'Why don't you call the police?'

'Seems to be a popular refrain. I might be crazy and she might merely be a working girl or some fool who has a crush on Leonard Card. But if she is the sniper I don't want the police to blow it. It could get back to Card. He seems capable of slipping through their hands. Or she might get lost in Chicago. That would take her less than half an hour. She has no identity. If she gets away, she might never be found.'

'So the only way any of this is done right is if you do it yourself?'

'I couldn't put it any different myself.'

The only sound for a while was the steady hum of the tires on the highway.

After several silent miles, Harold spoke: 'Extra pain and suffering seems cause enough for a more severe punishment.'

By the time they reached the turn-off for Kokomo, chain store America reared its ugly and welcomed head. Shanahan needed something to eat and Harold, who had nursed his thermos of coffee for hours, needed to make room for a refill.

154

Popping up out of the mostly flat barren winter fields were gas stations and fast-food joints made of brick and neon.

The two of them stood outside, Shanahan eating a fish sandwich, careful not to knock over his coffee resting on the trunk.

'Still almost two more hours of this before we turn around and see the same thing on the way back.' Harold looked up the road. 'What if she's not there?'

'I'm kind of hoping she isn't.'

'What?'

'You think I'm going to arrest her? Shoot her?' Shanahan asked.

'Why are we doing this?'

'To find out who she is, if she is the shooter. If she is, then we can connect most of the dots.'

'If not?'

'Maybe we learn something, maybe we don't. You know how this works. You remember, don't you?'

Harold didn't answer, which meant he understood. He didn't like it, but he understood.

'You've only got two days,' Harold said.

'I've got the rest of my life.'

'Not a big difference, is there?' Harold smiled and went to the driver's-side door.

Shanahan was reminded of Kowalski's comment at his house on White River that recent afternoon. Their talks usually evolved into universal themes. Death, being the most certain at the same time the most mysterious, was among them. On this occasion Kowalski quoted Voltaire on his deathbed. When asked by a priest if he would

155

renounce Satan, Voltaire said, 'Now, now my good man, this is no time to be making enemies.'

Shanahan made up his mind to be civil to Harold, despite the man's obvious disapproval. Could be bitterness. As an ex-cop, he probably resented Bailey hiring someone else, especially a PI, and more especially an old, broken PI. Harold had the qualifications. Why? Shanahan wondered why she didn't trust him.

'Maybe she'll let you take over if the case isn't resolved,' Shanahan said.

Harold said nothing, gave nothing away.

Out of the windows, the empty countryside kept repeating itself. Occasionally there were birds on a wire, a billboard, a barn, a clump of trees, a few black-and-white cows in no special hurry to be anywhere or do anything. Occasionally there was a truckload of hogs passing too closely on the left, the stench somehow squeezing through the closed windows.

'We're all on the road to somewhere,' Harold said. 'They say pigs are smart. Do you think they have any idea where they're going?'

Silence dominated the next hour.

'Ever shoot a woman, Harold?'

'I don't know if I've ever met anyone who invited so much disdain.'

'I'm honored. I know I have a talent for pissing people off, but I had no idea I'd reached the level of "inviting disdain." Kind of classy. Thanks, Harold.'

'Don't mention it. In fact, I'd appreciate it if you didn't mention much of anything.'

Harold's own disdain could have come about

naturally. Shanahan wasn't a team player and he spoke plainly – too plainly sometimes. But there was no doubt Jennifer Bailey's lack of appreciation for Harold's professionalism and the years he'd spent earning her trust contributed to his humiliation. To top it off, Harold was driving Shanahan around.

Oddly, it was because neither Bailey nor Shanahan minced their words that she went with Shanahan. He wasn't an employee. But there was nothing he could say to Harold to bridge the gap of resentment without creating more.

Shanahan left the floating world behind. He could sense the car coming to a stop, hear the turn signals, feel the turn. He opened his eyes to see the motel, Benzie's, slide past the car window.

'I wish *I* could get paid to sleep,' Harold said.

'You mind cruising the parking lot a few times?' Shanahan asked, ignoring the sarcasm. It was serious business now.

'A silver Malibu?' asked Harold.

'Right.' Harold remembered. A good sign.

'Not yet. I've been looking.'

'Could be in the field by the trailer,' Shanahan said.

'Or behind it.'

They circled the motel parking lot three times. Pickup trucks, beat-up vans and a variety of cars and SUVs, many of them silver. There was probably no better car to pick than a silver or gray, smallish sedan if the driver wanted to go unnoticed. That would certainly be something a hitman, or woman, would value. No late model Malibu on the lot.

'Drop me off in front, park to see that gap to the field, and be prepared for a quick getaway.'

Shanahan walked slowly around the motel. Slowly because he wanted to give Harold time to get settled and because, as an old friend used to say, 'his get-up-and-go got up and went.'

He moved even more slowly toward the opening in the bushes, an opening easily wide enough for a car. He saw the trailer. Pink. Small. Probably a one-bedroom. He'd been inside enough trailers to know the layout, especially as they were defined by the placement of the windows and doors. Living room on the far right, kitchen, bath, bedroom. There would be only two doors to the outside, both on the same side. One opened into the living room, the other the bedroom.

No light on inside. No tire tracks to indicate a car had pulled around back on a regular basis. She wasn't there. He looked at his watch. 3 p.m.

When she wasn't killing people, did she have a day job? Was she just out on an errand? Lunch?

He looked down at himself. He wished he looked a bit scruffier. If there were someone on the other side of the door, he could claim he was looking for work. Odd jobs. Handyman kinds of things.

There was no answer. He was insistent. If she was inclined to not answering in hopes the visitor would go away, he had to be irritating enough to make her come to the door to dismiss him. She wasn't there. With his left hand only partially connected to his brain, picking even this simple

158

lock was not a simple task. He dropped the pick twice.

Inside was almost as cold as outside. Apparently she conserved on heating bills. But that also meant she probably wasn't on a quick errand. Dirty avocado-colored dishes were in the sink. An empty beanie-weenie can was on the counter. The wastebasket was filled with empty Diet Coke cans. There was a blanket on the small sofa that faced a large flat-screen TV. Towels were carelessly hung in the shower area. The bed was unmade. She may be a perfectionist when it came to taking down her prey, but she wasn't a fastidious housekeeper.

Back in the kitchen, plastic plates and glasses in the upper cupboard. He struck it rich when he dropped to his haunches and opened the doors to the lower cupboard. Boxes of ammunition, oil, tools to clean weapons. In one of the drawers were a Glock and a couple of knives, binoculars and two scopes, one with a laser. In the tall, narrow cabinet beside the sink, tucked between broom and mop, were a standard .22 rifle and an M40, the US Marine sniper rifle.

She had minimal tools of the trade, but good choices.

Something hit him in the back, smashing his face against the edge of the cabinet. Something sharp pierced his jacket. Something climbed on his shoulder. Claws dug into the back of his neck and the back of his head, up to his neck, cutting into the flesh. Shanahan turned and twisted. He reached back with his good hand, feeling fur and muscle. He pulled twenty-five pounds of angry animal away, throwing it with as much force as he could. The cat hit the back of the sofa and bounced on the floor. It shot past him and into the bedroom.

Shanahan checked himself out in the bathroom mirror. His neck was scratched and bleeding. So were the backs of his hands. And his nose. The little sliver of ear shot off earlier by the cat's owner bled again. Shanahan looked more than a little roughed up. He pictured the cat in a little electric chair.

Shanahan was pretty sure the fierce feline wasn't trained to guard the trailer. It was merely batshit crazy.

He checked out the small medicine cabinet for something to sterilize the wounds. Nothing. Then again, the wounds were not serious. The medicine cabinet often offered great insight into its owner's character. No prescription painkillers. She was on the pill. Nothing else. If she had a stash of coke or weed, it would be hidden somewhere. Shanahan didn't care enough to look. And the cat just might be planning another attack. He made sure no one had pulled in then hurried back to the Lexus.

'Here,' Harold said, handing Shanahan a couple of tissues. 'Don't get blood on the upholstery.'

Shanahan used the outside mirror to clean up a little more.

'You run into Mike Tyson in there?' Harold asked as Shanahan slid into the backseat.

'A relative, maybe.'

What happened?'

'I'd rather not talk about it,' Shanahan said.

'And . . .?' Harold asked.

'She's our lady.'

'Where to?'

'Here.'

Shanahan went inside the motel. They still had a public phone. Lots of stuff went on here, he thought. Drugs, prostitution, probably gambling.

'Collins here,' came the voice.

'It's definite,' Shanahan said. 'Guns, ammunition. Night-scopes, day-scopes, laser-scopes. She's the shooter.'

'You better be right. We could invade a small country with what we've got ready. When?'

'I'll call. You want her in the trailer with it.'

Harold kept himself entertained with the electronic device he held in his hand. Shanahan made a couple of trips to the vending machines and drifted in and out of sleep, sitting up. The sun started dropping from the sky a little before five in the evening. It was dark by six.

Harold took turns with the car running and not. Keeping the edge off the chill.

'It's like we're at the drive-in,' Harold said. 'Most boring times in my life were waiting for the movie to begin. Ten more minutes to show time, it would say. And now I ask you, Shanahan, how many minutes until show time?'

There was no guarantee. She could have been off killing someone in Kansas City. The presence of the cat suggested she might return sometime soon.

'I don't know. I'm just hoping there is one.'

Cars pulled out. Cars pulled in. Some backed

161

in as Harold had. After six, there was a bit more traffic to watch in the parking lot. None of it Samantha.

The silver Malibu made the turn in the parking lot at an unwise speed, then made another into the opening that led to the trailer. Both Shanahan and Harold sat up straight. Shanahan started to exit when a white pickup truck, also speeding, made the same turns. Shanahan got out of the car, walked toward the gap into which the two vehicles disappeared. As he approached he heard doors shut, laughter, loud shouts in a kind of wahoo moment.

'Told you, you couldn't lose me,' said the male voice.

'What else are you good at?' the female voice shouted.

'You'll see, babe, I'll be right on your tail the rest of the way.'

The couple, a stringy blonde woman and a man with a slender build and a baseball cap, went inside. Shanahan heard the trailer door lock. Lights went on inside.

'Now what?' came a whispered voice in Shanahan's ear. Harold was beside him.

He gave Harold the numbers. Harold punched them in. Shanahan took the phone.

'Two of them,' he said. 'The girl and her boyfriend, probably a pick-up date. Doubt if he knows who he's dealing with. We're at Benzie's on US 31 South. The trailer, a single, pink trailer, is behind the motel in an open field, pretty good size. If she's spooked she can get lost in the farms and woodlands behind. She's a pro. She might

162

well have an escape plan. The entrance is through the motel's parking lot, a break in the high shrubs. Her Chevy and the guy's pickup are inside, almost blocking the front door of the trailer and tight just inside the entrance . . .

'Is there a back door?' Collins asked.

'Two doors in front. None in back. Only windows. We'll be here. You might want to come in quiet.'

Collins laughed. 'You have no idea.'

'When?' Shanahan asked.

'Five minutes.'

'What's up?' Harold asked.

'If you have to pee, do it now.'

Twenty-Two

The sound beating against Shanahan's chest nearly knocked him down, the bush branches reached out to slap at him, scratch him. The lights, from the night sky, directly above him, finally retreated, leveled. The trailer was lit like an encounter of the third kind, soon mixed with flashing red and blue of surrounding police cars and the pummeling beat of the chopper wings, bass for the whooping sirens.

The chopper had landed between the trailer and open country.

Three-dozen cops wearing shields, helmets and bulletproof vests pushed into the open field. A guy in a suit with a bulletproof vest came in close to Shanahan and Harold.

'You, Shanahan?'

'I called it in. Yeah, Shanahan.'

The guy nodded. 'Two inside, right.'

'The male probably doesn't know what's going on.'

'I've found that to be true on a number of occasions,' Harold said. 'I didn't know you had all this drama inside you.' He smiled, headed back to his car.

There was a rush inside the trailer. Lights flashed inside. There was shouting.

Collins came up to Shanahan after Samantha and her friend were sorted out. They were put in

164

separate squad cars. He looked to be eighteen, a know-it-all in for a rude awakening. She was a little older. She looked angry, but not frightened. People in blue jackets were taking the trailer down to its bones. Someone came up to the trailer with a cage. Looked like attack kitty might be arraigned for assault.

'Good work. Glad you were on our side,' Collins said.

'That takes care of who pulled the trigger, that's all,' Shanahan said. 'My guess is she'll hold it together better than Card. Without at least one of them, we can't get to the man pulling the strings.'

'Or woman,' Collins said. 'You want to ride with us? Get you home quicker.'

'Not this time,' Shanahan said, thinking he might be in line for sainthood – not leaving Harold behind – though in fact Harold might have preferred it.

'We're not setting a precedent here,' Maureen said, bringing him a shot of J.W. Dant bourbon and a glass of Guinness. 'How do you feel?'

'Surprisingly sleepy, considering I slept most of the way back. But I should be doing this for you. You found the trailer.'

A fire in the fireplace warmed the room, both in terms of temperature and of light.

'Tomorrow?' she asked.

'Theoretically, it's the last day of pay and of Harold. And I have no thoughts about next steps.'

'Some news. Might be good. Might not.'

He waited for her to continue.

165

'A few of the people who own property in the zone have signed an option to sell with Tyrus Investments.'

'That's great.'

'Well, maybe. They don't have any contact information. Kowalski found some as well. But . . .'

'Someone had to sign it for the corporation or it isn't valid,' Shanahan said.

'Halston Fournier.'

'What?'

'Halston Fournier.'

'Before he died?'

'That's what I'm guessing.'

'Don't smirk. In the criminal world dead men may not dance, but they might do things like vote or buy property.'

'Kowalski said that he believed Tyrus intervened when back taxes got to the point of confiscation,' Maureen said, 'and Tyrus offered creative solutions that enabled owners a chance to get something out of it.' She looked perplexed. 'But if Halston is dead?'

'That is the question. It was in his will or trust and went to Alexandra Fournier when his heart failed him. Alexandra, it appears, turned it over in some fashion to her brother, Charles, who was eliminated after receiving a substantial amount of cash, probably to turn over Tyrus to . . . whom? Daniel Holcomb, the videotape suggests. For how much? For what appears to be probably a pittance compared to what Tyrus is worth.' Shanahan took a sip of bourbon. 'What percentage of the landowners in the area do you think you and Kowalski talked to?'

'Not even a percentage. I managed to find ten or so who could even understand the question. Two came up with Tyrus. I think Kowalski got three. Top speed is ice age.'

'I see.'

'It's not likely they could or would even want to buy or take an option on it all. Just key properties here and there, without which a large, master development plan couldn't fetch such a price that people were killed over it.'

'You've been thinking about this.'

'I have. I feel like a tycoon,' Maureen said.

'Key properties, maybe used as leverage. Then option or buy up more as the plan develops,' Shanahan said.

'Or the judge was not as astute as we give him credit for. Or the value could be for one property,' Maureen added.

'What?'

'We saw this as a whole development plan incorporating various neighborhoods.'

There was no other indication that Charles was on some grand plan, just an amateurishly rendered map that may be no more than the beginning of a con for Charles. Sleep was about to overtake him. Shanahan tried to stay awake long enough to finish his thought. Buried in the list of generally worthless options was one real jewel. Someone knew it.

Morning was sudden for Shanahan. Not for Maureen. He was able to slip out without so much as a moan or a squirm from her luscious body on the other side of the bed. If his luck continued he'd get through his first cup of coffee and the morning newspaper before she flip-flopped down the hall.

A photograph of the helicopter and silhouettes of cops in helmets with shields occupied half the page above the fold of the *Indianapolis Star*. Shanahan imagined the same was true for the *South Bend Tribune*.

Shanahan read the short accompanying story:

> In a joint effort, the Indianapolis Metropolitan Police Department (IMPD) and the South Bend Police Department (SBPD), made an arrest in the sniper murders of Alexandra Fournier and her brother, Charles Bailey. IMPD Captain M. Anderson Collins said the suspect might be connected to another death as well. The arrest was made in a field behind Benzie's Motel on South Bend's far south side.
>
> The suspect was not named, but Collins said several firearms and a large quantity of ammunition were recovered, indicating they were correct to consider the arrest dangerous enough to use the SWAT strategy in the apprehension.

The coffee pot beeped. The toast popped up and the phone rang.

'I thought I'd give you the news,' Collins said.

'I've just read the news, you know, where you saved the earth from an asteroid.'

'No, the new news.'

'Shoot.'

'Leonard Card has been absolved of any wrong doing in the death of Justice King.'

'Do we know who voted what way?' Shanahan asked.

'That's not the way it works. They came to an agreeable statement that indicated that "evidence wasn't conclusive enough to offset his years of service," I'm reading now, "and the emotional and dangerous situation in which the officer acted."'

'That takes the heat off him for the Hernandez death as well, doesn't it?' Shanahan said. 'What about our friend Samantha? Maybe she can shed some light on Card.'

'We talked, she and I. Shanahan, she's tough. She's not new to this. She knows no one named Card. She shoots rabbit and duck, not people, she says. When she's not outright defiant she feigns confusion, but I doubt if we'll see a tearful confession. And I doubt if she'll flip.'

'How does she explain Card?'

'She doesn't. Doesn't know him. Never heard of him. Maybe you got the license plate wrong,' Collins said with more than a hint of sarcasm.

If Samantha was as tough as Collins said and Card, who had weathered two separate serious investigations and was toughened by years on the force in rough assignments, was equally unbreakable, where was the weak link?

Daniel Holcomb came to mind as he was about to get his toast and just as the phone rang again.

'Is it over?' Miss Bailey asked.

169

'As over as you want it to be,' Shanahan said. 'I think we have the actual killer of your sister and your brother. Proving it is another matter. I think we know who arranged the hits and who ordered them, but it might be difficult to prove.'

'I see.' There was a long pause. 'I believe the question I wanted answered when I hired you was: what was my sister coming to see you about? Do we have an answer to that?'

'I'm afraid it's all in the witch's brew. I have no idea . . .'

'You have no idea? I suspect you do,' Jennifer Bailey said. 'Justice King. He was a graduate of Second Chance. That's why she came to see you.'

Shanahan couldn't bring himself to break the long silence that followed.

'I'll send you a check,' she said finally. Her voice was hoarse, dry.

'You have what you want?' he asked.

'Yes. You did what I asked you to do,' she said.

'You know Leonard Card was essentially exonerated in the boy's death. He's a free man.'

'That's for the police now.'

'Miss Bailey, you miss the point here. Your sister's concerns haven't been addressed.'

'My sister's concerns aren't mine. I've found out what I set out to find. Thank you for your contribution.' She disconnected.

Maybe it was about the will for her. Maybe it was about Tyrus. Knowing was not enough for Shanahan. He wanted the person who hired the sniper to pay. That was true. Perhaps even more, he wanted Card. Even if King's death was unintended, the death of Hernandez wasn't.

170

Getting Card was the only way to diminish the haunting.

Coffee with toast and apple butter on an autumn morning. The sound of Maureen shuffling toward the kitchen, a slim ray of sun angling through a gap in the blinds all struggled to bring a little cheer to the morning. It wouldn't be enough.

He'd have to find a way to settle things.

Twenty-Three

Maureen reluctantly – she didn't want him out alone – dropped Shanahan off downtown so he could talk to Collins and get a look at Samantha, the hitwoman. Collins had agreed to meet him at the station before Samantha Byers was transferred to the Marion County Jail, only a few blocks away but more difficult to access. Shanahan would never have a chance to question her. On the other hand, he didn't need to. She was it. The only question that remained was whether or not she killed the kid.

Five foot two and 105 pounds at the most, Shanahan thought as he peered into a room occupied by Samantha, a dirty blonde and maybe someone fighting against the advance of her midthirties, and an oily man Shanahan presumed to be her lawyer.

'Where's her lawyer from?'

'Chicago.'

It was a shame, Shanahan thought. Kowalski would have loved to defend her, but even his tangential involvement in the case precluded it.

'She's a tough, wiry woman,' Collins said, 'but a garrote?'

Shanahan nodded. A sharp wire of any sort with a wood handle to leverage the twist would require less physical strength on the part of the attacker. He thought it possible but unlikely. The boy might not have been a linebacker but he was a well-built kid not quite twice her size who grew up in a tough neighborhood and who likely possessed the instinct to punch and kick. The other factor Shanahan thought about was that it was one thing for distance to turn killing into an abstraction and quite another to be up close and personal, actually feeling the life drain from the victim. Ask bomber pilots. Maybe drone operators.

'It was Card who killed the kid in the backyard,' Shanahan said.

'You can say it, even believe it . . .'

'What are you going to do?'

'We'll see if Annie Oakley will give us something.'

'In other words you don't mind there are murderers out there as long as the public thinks the case is closed.'

'I can't go after Card,' Collins said. 'The public committee cleared him. Internal Affairs signed off on their conclusion. He's back on duty. Anything more would be viewed as harassment. We are not going to keep on pursuing him based on suspicion. Maybe she'll break or make a deal. For now, we have to move along. It's over.'

They stood silent, facing each other. Collins broke the stand off. 'Some probably unwelcome advice: I understand your reputation for dogged determination and that you're not easily diverted, but don't take on Card. I know your history. And I know you can be tough. You can probably be mean. But you would be mean by necessity. Card, guilty or not, is mean by nature. Look at what he's done. Look at what he's gotten by with.'

'Too big to fail,' Shanahan said. He turned and walked away.

Daniel Holcomb kept Shanahan waiting well over forty-five minutes. Understandable. Shanahan had no appointment and refused to make one. At this point Holcomb had nothing to gain by seeing Shanahan. And he could lose billable hours. Fortunately the sofa in the waiting room was comfortable, the magazines up to date and the temperature pleasant enough. Shanahan didn't know how long it had been before the word 'Shanahan' pierced his dozing mind. He had to shake himself alert and stand still for a moment after he stood so the blood flow could catch up with him. A little feeble physically and mentally, he followed the woman into Holcomb's office. Whoever the attorney met with before Shanahan arrived had left through a different door – common law-office design, he imagined, when the business at hand was often between battling opponents.

'We can't keep meeting like this,' Holcomb said, smiling. It was a brief smile and his statement held more truth than humor. He stood directly in front of Shanahan, a clear indication he wasn't being invited to stay.

'I see you understand the nuances of body language.'

'I've made commitments to other people.'

'People who are paying you for your time.'

'Precisely,' Holcomb said.

'You were uncomfortable when Swann came into the committee room to testify.'

'And how do you know that?'

'I'm a professional investigator.' Shanahan wasn't sure he'd ever said it that way. But Holcomb was using subtle intimidation to shrug off Shanahan's questions. And it might have gotten Shanahan equal footing, at least for a moment. Holcomb relaxed, stepped back.

'I was extremely disappointed. I thought the hearing was nearing an end. And when I saw it was a policeman, a plainclothes policemen, it seemed like all hope was thrown overboard, the case would go on forever and I'd get all tied up with meaning-less crap, excuse the language, like this.' It was clear he was referring to the current conversation.

'Surprised Card too.'

'I noticed that. We all expected the witness wouldn't be so reputable.'

'Yet you pretty much took him apart, this repu-table witness.'

'What are you trying to say, Mr Shanahan?'

'You acted as Card's personal defense attorney, Mr Holcomb.'

'Instinct. I am a defense attorney. It's the way I get to the truth.'

'Did you?'

'In the same imperfect way American justice works.'

'You were also in possession of knowledge about Swann's presence at the event in question that had not been discussed in your meetings, that had not appeared in any reports or transcripts you were given.'

'Really, and how do you know all this?' Holcomb asked, already heading for the door. He opened it. 'Look, people talk,' he said, 'in hallways, public restrooms and over drinks at the bar. If you remember, I was the one who first mentioned the Card case. I told *you* about it. Why would I do that if I were involved in some nefarious conspiracy with the man? And what do you think I'm getting from Card? I don't even like the guy.'

'Do you know a woman named Samantha Byers?' Shanahan asked, stopping in the doorway.

'I know what the newspaper says.'

'You represent rich criminals, you said. Does that mean organized crime?'

'I'm not sure there is such a thing, Mr Shanahan. Just business and variations on greed. Some take more risks than others. I try to help judges and district attorneys interpret the rules.' He stepped back. 'You may have all day to chat . . .'

'I have a library to visit, old news to look up, connections to make.'

There was no offer to shake hands.

He hadn't upset Holcomb as much as he'd wanted. Then again, keeping cool was something Holcomb practiced regularly. No matter. If the young, rich and handsome attorney was involved, the pot was stirred. If he wasn't involved, then Shanahan had made a grand fool of himself. At this point, that was the only thing Shanahan could do. Not much to lose, was there? Shanahan asked himself.

* * *

The walk from Holcomb's office near the copper glass-covered box that was the City-County Building (City Hall) to the library was seven or eight blocks. Flat, thank God, interrupted, further thanks to God, by memorials and parks with benches. This area was the most monumental area of a city devoted to monuments.

Shanahan put the library visit off to eat a slice from Datsa Pizza. The place used to be a Toddle House years ago, Shanahan remembered. Still had the same blue-tiled roof. The Ambassador Apartments were across the street, a large building with tons of charming, little studios. He had had some business in a couple of them over the years. The Ambassador had been renovated with some folderol not that long ago, as had the library. The original book palace was a handsome building of formal Greek architecture. That stately building now sat in front of an expanded gigantic glass mirrored addition. The formidable library capped several block-long memorials to dead soldiers.

Shanahan climbed the grand steps as a man who possessed more time than energy, yet he felt he had little of either. He entered the building, past the sculptures, between the Doric columns, through various sets of old doors into an old interior. Inside was as before. He could see into the next room, huge, new and full of color. It was a strange feeling. He felt a hand clutch his shoulder, stopping him.

'You're coming with me,' the voice said. They were outside again. He had been pulled back. Shanahan turned. It was Card. He was in his blues. One hand remained at Shanahan's neck, the other on his .45, holster already unsnapped. This was a public performance. It didn't matter. Shanahan wasn't strong enough to resist.

'My heart,' Shanahan said as loud as he could and still appear feeble. He clutched his chest.

They stopped at the top of the steps. Fat slices of snow fell, slowly and feebly as the last of the confetti falls after the parade is over.

Shanahan put one foot in front of Card's ankle and pulled his head free while pushing as hard as he could on Card's back.

Twenty-Four

In a blue blur the man was gone, falling, tumbling, sliding down the steps amid the scattering gasps. Shanahan turned back, quickly entering the library, and headed to a historically preserved room just off the entry.

Shanahan found himself in a nice office. He took the wrinkled trench coat off the coat rack, the scarf, and the umbrella that could easily double as a walking stick or weapon. He stole the hat too and went back the way he came, this time walking up the steps and into the new, modern space. Card had recovered and limped quickly into the vast space. The angry cop, somewhat disheveled, his mad eyes dismissing the newly formed Shanahan, came within a few feet of his disguised prey.

Shanahan ducked down to a side door. He walked south on Meridian, catching a glimpse of himself in the mirrored exterior wall of the library's new addition. He looked like some old, stylized private eye. For a moment he found humor in life's absurdities and took a moment of pride in having been so clever in giving Card the slip. He crossed St Clair and stood near the Tomb of the Unknown Soldier to see Card leave. The cop had called no back-up. No cops came to help him search. This was personal and Card wanted to keep it that way. In fifteen minutes

Card came back out of the main door, descended the steps and got into a squad car. Lights flashed. A siren screamed. Tires peeled. Card threw a tantrum. Shanahan's lightness of being brought about by a momentary triumph in the library gave way to a reality too heavy to dismiss. He'd gone too far. He'd poked Card's reptilian brain. That put not only his life in greater danger, but also Maureen's.

As the adrenaline dipped and his mind cleared, he realized he had told Holcomb where he was going. That Card knew to find him in the library confirmed the connection between the two. Not too bright of Holcomb or Card. On second thought, Shanahan decided, it was probably Card who jumped the gun.

Shanahan crossed the street, up the library steps, back into the office he had slipped off to. There was a man with a beard, thinning hair, thick glasses, a tweed coat and a camel cashmere V-neck sweater. Shanahan took off the borrowed overcoat, hung it on the hook, unwrapped the scarf, folded it and put it in the overcoat's pocket. He put the hat on top of the stand, carefully. The man didn't speak until Shanahan nodded a sort of 'Thank you.'

'Anything else I can do for you?' the man asked.

'Now that you mention it, may I use your phone?'

Kowalski and Collins met Shanahan at the City Market. It was just past lunchtime so the walk-ways between booths were without bustle. Kowalski held a cup of coffee, his body relaxed. Collins stood facing Shanahan.

'I know you don't want to hear it,' Shanahan said, 'but Card has turned into a mad dog.'

'Kowalski told me what you say happened. Sounds like resisting arrest, if you ask me. Assault.'

'So then he called in, asked for back-up to apprehend a perp who assaulted him and got away?' Kowalski took a sip of coffee.

Collins said nothing.

'C'mon Collins, give it up. You have a rogue cop on your hands,' Kowalski said.

Shanahan's legs were weak and wobbly from walking back. He headed toward the front to find a place to sit.

'The only person who knew I was going to the library was Daniel Holcomb,' Shanahan said, 'the person who helped him skate on charges of killing some innocent kid.'

'I've got to get back to work,' Collins said. 'I'll have a chat with Card.'

'Yeah, give him a time out,' Shanahan said. 'The sniper's car was in Card's driveway. They're connected.'

'Yeah, yeah, like your memory is going to hold up in court.' Collins headed toward the door.

'Harold will testify to that,' Shanahan said. 'How do you think I located Samantha? Harold got her address from her car in his driveway.'

Collins kept going until his phone beeped. He stopped.

'You and Maureen can come up to my place to hide out,' Kowalski said.

Collins came back, his face unreadable.

'Samantha Byers no longer exists,' he said. 'Swann got a call.'

'How?' Shanahan asked.

'Shiv. It happened in the john. I told Swann to send some uniforms out to pick him up.'

'When?' Shanahan asked.

'Just an hour or two ago.'

'They get who did it? Shanahan asked.

Collins shrugged. 'Nobody saw anything.'

'Did Card have her killed? Or was Card's attack on me a reaction to Samantha's death?' Shanahan asked.

'Or did Holcomb worry about too many people knowing what had happened?' Kowalski added.

'Anyone besides you he might be after?' Collins asked.

'Maureen, for spite,' Shanahan said.

'Find a safe place,' Collins said.

'Great advice. No wonder you've gotten so far.'

Collins was too concerned about current events to be bothered with the sarcasm. He had a more serious problem. Cop on cop. 'We'll work it out, Shanahan. Don't provoke him. You're off the case anyway, right? Go find a cabin on a mountaintop.'

Collins disappeared.

'Have you eaten?' Kowalski asked.

Shanahan nodded. 'Is there a way to get a list of Daniel Holcomb's clients?'

'That would be fun.'

'And useful,' Shanahan added.

'Why don't you have Maureen go up to my place now?' Kowalski pulled out his cell. 'What's her number?'

Shanahan told him. Kowalski poked at the

numbers, listened for a moment and handed the phone to Shanahan.

'Kowalski wants you to sleep at his place tonight.'

'Oh?' Maureen said.

'He and I made a deal.'

'How much did you get?'

After calling Maureen, Shanahan brought Jennifer Bailey up to date. He didn't have to, but he thought she was entitled to know. And he wanted to keep that lifeline open in case he needed it. Not knowing the mind of the increasingly crazed cop, she needed to know he was not to be trusted.

Kowalski lived in Ravenswood, another one of those neighborhoods – Woodruff Place and Beech Grove – that maintained an independent attitude toward the city that surrounded them. Ravenswood residents, more than the others, regard those they don't know with suspicion and are not generally fond of outside authority – cops, for example. Harley-riding James Fenimore Kowalski fit in perfectly.

'There's a shotgun in the closet by the back-door,' he said to Shanahan and Maureen as part of the welcome speech. They had been to Kowalski's place a few times, but not always when they were under siege. 'There's a nine millimeter behind *Last of The Mohicans* on the bookshelf here,' he said, pointing to the classic on a shelf near the front door. And an M14 in the closet in the upstairs hall. You'll be sleeping up there. You know the M14?'

'I do,' Shanahan answered. That was still the standard issue rifle when he retired.

'All weapons are loaded, so be careful,' Kowalski said. 'Also,' he continued as he headed for three glasses and a bottle of Scotch, 'there's an outboard tied up at the dock down from the back door.'

'You ever thought of raising an army?' Shanahan asked, while Kowalski poured two fingers of Scotch into Maureen's glass.

'Or a navy,' Maureen said.

'I'm sorry. No rum,' he said to Maureen. 'I'll get some in.'

'I'm hoping to wrap all of this up pretty quick,' Shanahan said.

Kowalski was a good host. He put on some music, starting with 'Gloomy Sunday' and 'Nightmare,' both performed by Artie Shaw.

'It will lighten up,' Kowalski assured them. Chardonnay and roasted chicken for the evening. He shoed Maureen from the kitchen with a refill of the Scotch.

'When we go, we will feel no pain,' she said.

'That's the idea. It's also important to keep labor at a minimum. By the way, the secret to roast chicken is that there is no secret to roast chicken. Just roast the damned thing,' he said. 'Now, how about a little roasted human?' He went to the fireplace and set the stack of wood newspapers on fire.

'Good idea,' Shanahan said. 'We don't want the chicken to have all the fun.'

'Here's the list of Holcomb's clients,' Kowalski said, dodging his bulldog, who waddled toward Maureen. She had settled near the fireplace to

184

hand some papers to Shanahan. 'Plenty of big names, but not those you'd expect to find on a list of criminals.

'In most situations, the indictments don't come down, especially if the attorney is up to snuff. No one even knows there were criminal inquiries. Sometimes a deal, usually in the form of a fine, is struck. All hush-hush. Sometimes, before entering a deal, a corporation will call in the appropriate attorney for advice on how to do what they want to do without chancing arrest.'

Shanahan scanned the list again. Some names gave no clue to the kind of business they were: holding companies that owned holding companies. He did recognize a hotel, realtors, developers, a publisher, venture capitalists and a number of politicians. It wasn't particularly helpful. On the surface no individual or company fit. And there was the chance that Holcomb was doing some business on his own.

'The morose music is apropos,' Shanahan said. 'I'll never be able to make sense of all this.'

'I'm not sure someone like Holcomb would tap a low-life like Card unless he felt he had no choice. He may be morally challenged, but he's not stupid,' Kowalski said.

'I'm not sure I can sleep,' Maureen said in the darkness. 'In a way I hope so . . . it's not home.'

'You slept in Hawaii.'

'I did. That doesn't count.'

'Why not?'

'Hawaii is a sleeper's paradise. The waves, the sun, the breeze.'

'Close your eyes and pretend you are in Hawaii,' Shanahan said.

'You think I can't talk with my eyes closed?'

'Give me some credit.'

'Do you think Card blames you for Samantha's death?'

'In a way, I hope so.'

'You really hate him, don't you?'

'I've never hated anyone.'

'Until now,' Maureen said.

'I hated Hitler, but never someone I knew, and I've run into some not very nice people over the years. Other people have tried to kill me. It was business.'

'Business?'

'Nothing personal. Card killed someone who was doing good for people who needed help. Card killed a kid and I believe he took gratification from a senseless act.'

What he didn't say was that in those days before Maureen, he didn't have the fear of losing her. It wasn't just *his* life in the balance.

'Aloha,' she said.

Daylight came slowly on overcast fall mornings. The air was thick with cold and dampness. That much Shanahan could see through the bedroom window. He dressed, slipping into his shoes without untying them. Untying them wasn't the problem. Tying them with his half-dead left hand was nearly impossible. He'd have to wait until Maureen got up so he could stand there like a two-year-old while she did it.

Scrambled eggs, bacon, coffee. Kowalski was

an attentive host even without a couple of glasses of whiskey. Shanahan thought the lawyer's coffee was suspect, though.

'Go look out the front door,' he said with a half-smile that suggested Shanahan was about to see something extraordinarily funny or extraordinarily grotesque.

Shanahan did. A police car, a black-and-white, was parked out front.

'Are we having company for breakfast?'

'The front door on the driver's side was open. Footprints in the frost indicated the driver had walked around the house. Just before making a complete circle, another set of footprints, slightly larger, intersected with the first. Both continued to the water's edge. Both disappeared.'

Kowalski poured Shanahan a cup of coffee.

'I called Collins. He's on his way out.'

'Anything else?'

'My boat has gone.'

Twenty-Five

'What do you know?' Kowalski asked Collins as he came in. Collins glanced at Shanahan, who was putting some apricot preserve on his toast, and then up at Maureen as she descended the stairs.

'You have a license for a bed and breakfast?' Collins asked.

'Lose a car?' Kowalski said in response.

'Lost a cop, I think,' Shanahan said.

Kowalski explained the footprints, the missing boat.

'Someone was outside last night?' Maureen asked.

'No prints now,' Collins said.

'Frost. Kind of like looking for fingerprints on an icicle,' Kowalski said. 'They were there fifteen minutes ago.'

Collins pulled out his cell. 'Tell Swann to come on out and bring the kids in the white coats.' He put the phone back. 'Some blood splatter on a rock.'

'Is that Card's squad car?' Shanahan asked.

Collins nodded. 'Signed out to him.'

'You don't know where he is?' Shanahan asked.

'No contact at all yesterday. Sent someone to his place. Nothing. And some other news. The girl, Samantha, may not have been murdered. She may have done the deed herself. We're looking into it.'

'So he may not have ordered her hit to protect himself?' Shanahan asked.

'Even monsters can fall in love,' Maureen said. 'Maybe he loved her.'

Shanahan said nothing, but he didn't believe a broken heart was in Card's nature. Revenge, maybe. Personal survival would rate high on a list of motives.

No one else spoke. It was clear that not only was there nothing to say, but that no one knew what to do. Card was the essential link. If he was disposed of, they would all be back to zero.

'What time did she die?' Shanahan asked.

'Early morning.'

'He could have tailed me down to Holcomb's office and then to the library. He was in a rage. Her death could be why.' Shanahan said. 'He had to know where I lived so he could tell her where Fournier could be shot.' Then he remembered. 'I told him where I was going,' Shanahan said.

'Who?' Kowalski asked.

'Holcomb. Like I said before, I told him I was going to the library to look up all sorts of things. Largely a bluff to make him nervous. I can't believe I forgot.'

'And you did make him nervous,' Collins said. 'And you may be next on this endless list.'

Shanahan had to find a safer place for Maureen, a safe method to get her there. And, most difficult of all, convince her to go. If Card was alive, then he probably still wanted Shanahan dead. If Card blamed Shanahan for Samantha's death – if he cared at all – Maureen might also be a target. If Card was dead as the scene suggested, or as it was intended to imply, his killer might well believe Shanahan had incriminating information and must be eliminated as well. Death seemed to be the solution to everything. Wasn't it? he asked himself.

Shanahan would return to his home and play the role of the tethered goat. He understood he had no client. He had no moral responsibility. In fact, a good case could be made for him to stay out of it. Go off to Hawaii. He realized, though, he could not let this go. He couldn't go on even with his petty, uneventful life with the dead boy's picture still in his head.

'Did Holcomb decide to take Card out? 'Shanahan asked. 'If so, how did he find the people to do the job?'

'Everyone who knew anything has been killed,' Kowalski said. 'The killer – the person calling the shots, that is – is pretty thorough, pretty paranoid.'

Kowalski stepped outside to watch the crime scene investigators arrive. Collins was already out there.

'And then there was one,' Maureen said. She shrugged. 'I don't know what that means. It just came out.'

'You're crazier than I thought,' Maureen said when Shanahan suggested she slip on one of the crime scene investigators' white coats from their lab, go to the airport and catch a plane to California where Shanahan's son and family lived. They'd love to have her. 'No,' she said firmly.

190

'When this is over, I'll join you. A little vacation in wine country?'

'No. Your brain is on the fritz. Even your left side is iffy. You can't tie your shoes. You've broken half our china . . .'

'Maureen, I'm a professional,' he said, half believing it but wholeheartedly wanting to. 'I don't tell you how to sell a house. I don't demand to be there when you're closing the deal. That is what you do. This is what I do.'

He thought he might have gotten through, but he hadn't.

'There's a time,' she said.

'Crap,' he said.

He knew. When he sat down to pay his bills, even his right hand did not follow directions. His handwriting had become illegible. Trying to stuff checks and bills into envelopes became a challenge. The scrunched-up envelopes looked like his hands, not only wrinkled but slightly contorted. The whole process took longer, much longer, frustratingly longer. He moved slower, thought slower. But, even in poor shape, he would stand a better chance if he didn't have to worry about her as well as himself. He could figure out a way to compensate for his shortcomings. What made her presence problematical is that in these kinds of circumstances he would never be able to accurately predict her behavior. And he would be more concerned about protecting her than doing his job, which was to kill the bastard.

She was right. He was right. Yet they were going in completely different directions. He needed to do what he needed to do. Alone.

'This isn't negotiable,' she said.

'There's no room for error,' Shanahan said. While he was at the edge of the actuarial table, she had plenty of room. 'Listen to me. With my life the risk is low. I can't lose much. You can.'

'He may be dead, anyway,' Kowalski said, coming into the kitchen. 'It may be over.'

'He's not dead. It's not over.'

'How's that?' Kowalski asked. 'He have an accomplice? There were two sets of footprints. I saw them.'

Kowalski, shaking his head, draped Maureen's coat over her shoulder. Shanahan noticed it hung heavier on the right side. Maureen apparently noticed too. She put her hand in her pocket then pulled it out, trying to put a blank look on her face. Her poker face was always comical, Shanahan thought.

'Collins is having them match Card's DNA with the blood on the rock,' Kowalski said, 'and I overheard him telling someone to get a boat down here to check out the riverbank and, if necessary, drag the river for a body.'

'It will be Card's but they'll never find the body. Collins is wasting his time.'

Collins came up. 'Don't take my name in vain.' He looked at Shanahan. 'Until we find out what's going on here, why not take a vacation?' he asked, his eyes moving from Shanahan to Maureen. He smiled at the obvious defeat of his suggestion. 'I can have the area around your place patrolled.'

Uncomfortable quiet followed. 'Stay away,' Shanahan finally said.

'The problem is that if Card has been murdered,' Collins said, 'then there's another murderer to be found. Maybe two if Samantha didn't do herself in.'

'There always was,' Shanahan said. 'Card and Samantha were the hired help.'

He didn't tell them how much he wanted Card.

'Any other words of wisdom?' Collins asked.

'Daniel Holcomb.'

'The defense attorney?' Collins asked. 'In what way?'

'As I've said before, he seemed to be on Card's side in committee deliberations. He has expensive upkeep.'

'Not much. This is why there are twelve people on a jury. Oh, and your little Tyrus thing? How is that going?' Collins said as he left them.

Back home, he looked at the house differently. With the exception of the kitchen, which was the center of action. Shanahan read his morning paper there. Maureen, when she worked at home, set up her laptop there. Breakfast, lunch and dinner were consumed there. The table was for food and for work and for conversation. There were four doors in the kitchen: from the garage, to the basement, from the outside, and a doorway into the rest of the house.

The only other door from the outside was the front door, which opened into an entry hall. To the left was a hall to the two bedrooms and the bath. Other than these doorways, the only way in and out of the house was through windows. Shanahan nailed shut all of the windows that

193

couldn't be seen from the street. He nailed shut the door from the garage to the kitchen and used a padlock piece of hardware to secure the door from the kitchen to the outside.

'Lunch?' Maureen asked as Shanahan came up from the basement carrying a shopping bag full of J.W. Dant bourbon and Mount Gay rum. She had put away the groceries they picked up on the way home. Her eyes widened. 'I see we're setting priorities. What are you doing?'

He set the bag on the table, picked up the hammer and a nail the size of a railroad spike. As best he could with his half useless left hand, he drove the nail into the doorframe, sealing off the basement.

'Seems like we ought to be on Key Largo, the way we are battening down the hatches. Are we preparing for a hurricane?'

'We're preparing for a madman, professionally trained to carry out his madness.'

In the quiet that followed, Shanahan heard the raindrops hit the window. It would be a cold rain which, Shanahan thought, suited his closing up the house in anticipation of danger.

'I don't understand,' she said. 'Seems as if you're making some random choices. This door, but not that one. This window, but not . . .'

'When you're herding cattle, you funnel them into one exit. You limit their choices. I'm limiting Card's choices.'

'If I were him, I'd just burn down the house.'

'As a cop, he'd know better than that. Too iffy. He needs to know I'm dead.'

'That *we're* dead.'

'Maybe he'll just want you dead so I'll suffer,' Shanahan said.

'How sweet of you.'

Shanahan continued. He hid weapons – steak knives, a baseball bat, an aerosol can with a butane lighter – in various places around the house.

The day passed under the sparse, cold rain. With Shanahan's new ability to drift in and out of sleep in what seemed like a blink of an eye, he did not know how long he slept for. But he and Maureen were still alive when he decided to get out of bed at a dark six a.m. He didn't turn on any lights.

He pushed the button to get the coffee going. He looked out of the front window. Nothing to see. The newspaper, in a plastic bag, was just outside the front door.

Sitting at the kitchen table so that he'd be out of the line of fire, he read:

Missing Police Officer Feared Dead Indianapolis Metropolitan Police Department (IMPD) Sergeant Leonard B. Card, 53, has not communicated with his superiors in 48 hours. His squad car was found abandoned in Ravenswood yesterday under suspicious circumstances. Blood was found nearby. Authorities are testing DNA to determine if the blood belongs to Card.

Not much, Shanahan thought. When he turned the page he found a handwritten note that had

195

been tucked in: *You and your lovely Maurie enjoy the last minutes of your lives.*

Shanahan called Kowalski.

'Do you have a sadistic rooster over there?' Kowalski asked groggily.

'Sorry.' Shanahan brought the lawyer up to date, including the note inside the morning paper.

'You want me in the spare bedroom for a couple of days?'

'No, but could you do a complete background on someone?'

Kowalski agreed, though he was surprised by the name.

'Are you serious?'

'I am.'

Shanahan went to the bedroom. Maureen was asleep and curled up the way he had left her. He made the rounds of the house, in what little light the morning chose to provide. He checked his work. All seemed secure.

If Card wanted to disappear and start a new life, why would he write a note? He couldn't help it, Shanahan concluded. In a way, they were alike. Shanahan could have dropped the case. He had done what had been asked of him. In fact, he had been formally dismissed.

Maureen awoke. 'What happened to the heat?' She had draped herself in a blanket. She looked malformed and forlorn, a strange combination of monster and mood.

'I've already turned it up.' He poured a cup of coffee for her, stuffed the note in his pocket. 'It will catch up.'

By mid-morning it was clear. As the sun rose,

the temperature dipped. There was no catching up.

It occurred to her first: the situation was more serious than they wanted to admit. They were on the verge of an ice storm. If it happened, there was a good chance the electricity would go out. They had enough food and, clearly, they had enough alcohol. The refrigerator was unnecessary in such circumstances. The stove was gas. But light and communication with the outside world – TV, radio and some telephones – were at risk. Telephone lines were known to snap under the weight of constantly accumulating ice. She instantly put her cell phone in its charger.

She left the kitchen. When she returned, she was dressed. Warmly. She held out a sweater for Shanahan.

'Put this on,' she said.

'It's scratchy and it's a turtleneck.'

'It would seem silly to have saved your brain only to have you kick off with pneumonia,' she said.

He might have resisted more if he wasn't so cold.

'I need to get batteries, candles, a battery operated radio,' she said.

'No.'

'I have to go and I have to go now. It will only get worse.'

'I can't let you go out there. Who knows where Card is lurking.'

'The longer we wait the worse it gets.'

He followed her into the garage, having pulled out the nail that sealed it shut.

She kissed him on the cheek. 'Don't worry. I'm still packing.' She patted the pocket of her overcoat. 'I'm not afraid to use it,' she said, no doubt, Shanahan thought, trying to reassure both of them.

He stood just inside the door as she backed the car out. There was no real light, though it was just after noon. There were only dark shadows in a gray mist as far as the eye could see. The rain, though not yet dense, was hard and cold. It wouldn't be long before it turned to a torrent, coating everything with ice.

If it happened, the city would simply shut down. Cops, firefighters, emergency health workers – all would be stymied at least for a few hours. The night would be dark, everywhere.

He waited until she was on the street and moving forward before he pushed the button for the garage door to close. He was inside when he heard the door come to rest on the concrete.

Twenty-Six

Inside, in the kitchen, the first thing he saw was her cell phone getting re-energized in the wall outlet. She didn't have it with her. He put his half-cup of coffee in the microwave and went to the living room window to look out. Nothing had changed in the last few seconds.

He thought he heard a creaking sound, but if so, it was soon obliterated by the buzz of the microwave. He was on hyper alert, perhaps because he was worried about Maureen. Her going out. Leaving her cell behind. And a madman being loose. His being less than whole.

The phone rang.

'Shanahan.'

'This is Collins.'

'What's up?'

'The blood on the rock is Card's.'

'That was quick.'

'We had his on file. We had support from the top. Also, we found blood in the boat, which was floating around Broad Ripple Park.'

'Are you going to dredge?' Shanahan asked.

'He's dead,' Collins said.

'I have a theory,' Shanahan said.

'Let it go, Shanahan. You're like a terrier with a pant leg.'

'Who killed him?' Shanahan asked.

'That's for us to find out.'

'He's not dead.'

'Get some rest.' Collins disconnected.

As Shanahan put the phone down he noticed the plastic daily pill container. He hadn't taken his morning pills. He'd have to pay more attention. He took his morning dose: prednisone, a steroid prescribed to fight against the swelling and inflammation of his brain; two blood pressure pills; a pill for vitamin D and calcium; and the most important, two anti-seizure pills. He'd have a little dip in energy in a few minutes. He sipped some coffee to ward off a drift into naptime, then went to the window in the living room. He hoped Collins was right and Card was swirling into some black hole in space, but he couldn't ignore the note. He still wanted Maureen home. Now. The wind picked up and slammed the rain against the glass. The sky went battleship gray. Nearly black. He left the lights off to limit visibility from the outside.

There was a loud snap. The darkness was intensified but not complete. It was almost like the light suddenly dimmed in his brain. The room felt empty and dark. He felt empty and dark. His left hand began to jump on its own. He could see, but it was like looking through a veil. He was surprised to see Leonard Card in the kitchen doorway. Shanahan's .45 was in a drawer in the kitchen, on the other side of Card. No. Card was holding it.

The man with the gun seemed almost an apparition, a faint projection into the fog. In fact, the world seemed as if the light had been squeezed from it. Reality was in question.

'You know how to handle a forty-five, Card? You sissies on the force now have these nine millimeters; popguns for thirteen-year-old girls. Then you pick your victims carefully. A couple of adolescent boys and . . .'

'And an old geezer who should have checked out years ago.'

'After you, I'm probably next in line.'

Shanahan confirmed he could move his right arm normally. He could move his left arm, though he could not completely control its movement. All the while, his left hand continued to flip about like a dying fish. If he remembered correctly, his body, the whole left side of it, would soon do the same.

'How about that weather?' Shanahan asked.

'I was thinking of moving to a warmer climate,' Card said. He stepped into the living room.

'I suspect you'll eventually make it.' Shanahan didn't see how he could come out of this alive. But he had to find a way to keep Maureen from walking into her death.

'Your little friend, Maurie? Will she be home soon?'

Maurie. Shanahan thought of the note. His left eye twitched. Again. He was running out of time. He walked to the window.

'Stay still, Shanahan.'

'No one can see in,' Shanahan said, picking up the glass ashtray from the table beside the sofa.

'What are you doing, Shanahan?'

'Thought maybe you wanted to smoke.'

'I don't smoke.'

'No?' Shanahan turned and flung it against and through the window, breaking out nearly a third of it.

'What . . . Oh. Clever. Doesn't change much. If I don't do her here and now, I'll do her somewhere else, some other time.'

'Sounds like a song.' Shanahan wondered if Card could see the twitching at all. It wasn't just the left eye now, but the left side of the head.

'Stop it!' Card yelled.

'What?'

'Whatever trick you're trying to pull . . .' Card moved in. Cold and wet air whooshed through the hole in the window with each gust of the wind. 'It's not going to work.'

'The person who hired you will give you up.'

'No, she won't. You don't understand the dynamics here.'

Electric shock travelled down Shanahan's left side. He was being taken over by a greater force than Card. The man with the gun was becoming an afterthought. Any moment, Shanahan believed, it would all go dark and silent. Certainly he'd not be able to stand. His left knee jerked about.

'Did you love Samantha?' Shanahan managed to say, though the words came out twisted by his faulty brain. He didn't recognize his own voice.

Shanahan went down. His body lurched and jerked violently. He couldn't breathe, but he could still see, could still hear. Card cursed.

'You'll die like the boy did,' Card said. The cop was down with Shanahan. He had put the .45 aside and had the garrote in his hands. 'The police will connect the murders – you, Maurie and the kid in the backyard – but not with me.'

Shanahan tried to ask him again about Samantha, but the words came out gibberish. He understood it was gibberish, tried again and gave up, concentrating instead on breathing. It wasn't happening. Air was in short supply even before the wire slipped around his neck.

'I really wanted you to see me do her.'

Shanahan was being electrocuted and strangled. Neither of them worked. He was conscious, in pain and now making sounds he didn't know a human could make. Even so, he blessed his Maureen for encouraging him to wear a thick wool turtle-neck sweater.

Using his legs and hips on his right side, he flipped his body. Card was still trying to adjust his killing wire when Shanahan struck. With his jerking, crab-like left arm, he went for Card's neck. His fingers closed and locked in place, tightening on the front part of Card's throat. Card, eyes wide, hit Shanahan on the chest, on his face, on his side. All over his body crazily, at first with fury and then with hysteria. All the while Shanahan's body lurched, jumped, and flailed about, legs going one way, arms another. He didn't feel Card's punches. Card

203

changed his strategy. He had to. He was being strangled. His windpipe was being crushed, Card tried frantically to break free, no doubt to retrieve the .45. But with each shock, Shanahan's claw gripped tighter.

Twenty-Seven

At some point his memory stopped. The last Shanahan remembered he was convulsing on the floor and Card was trying to kill him. He didn't remember anything about the hospital or the room that he was in, brightly lit, clean and quiet.

For a moment he thought of nothing other than the state of his being. His fingers found bandages on his face, stitches on his lips. His chest was wrapped in gauze and he felt a subtle, low-level pain in his chest as he took breaths. There was a rubber tip attached to one of his fingers and a needle in his lower arm near his left wrist. Two clear bags, one no doubt containing saline and the other, a smaller one, probably a painkiller. It was with a sort of robotic intelligence that he took inventory and evaluated his environment. He thought of Maureen and his dissociative thoughts dissolved into panic.

Fortunately, she appeared. Behind her was Harold. Jennifer Bailey's Harold.

She kissed him on the forehead.

'You really are a tough old bird,' she said.

'Ditto, except for the kiss,' Harold said.

'Card?' Shanahan asked.

'Dead,' Harold said.

Shanahan looked at Maureen, sad that she would bear that burden.

'I shot him,' Harold said. Apparently seeing

205

the confusion on Shanahan's face, he added, 'Miss Bailey asked me to check on you now and then. I saw the window. Didn't have anything else to do.'

'Thank you,' Shanahan said. But he couldn't help looking into Harold's eyes for something that would help Shanahan believe him. Card's death would help the person who ordered the deaths of Mrs Fournier and her brother.

'I'll leave you two alone,' Harold said. 'Miss Bailey said she's glad it's over and for you to get well.'

Sometimes he wished he didn't have such a suspicious mind. But that's who he was. On the other hand, having Harold look in from time to time wasn't out of character for Jennifer Bailey. She wasn't the most warm-hearted person in the world, but she took responsibility more seriously than most. And she was thorough.

'The doctor said you'd be released this afternoon,' Maureen said. 'Aside from being pummeled pretty badly, your convulsion went on a while. You need a little rest.'

'What time is it?'

'A little after ten a.m. A day has passed,' she said, and sat on the edge of the bed. 'Do you need anything?'

'Not at the moment.' He had no idea of what he needed or might need. He was still adjusting to the new reality, whatever that was. 'I'm happy enough seeing you here.'

'I feel bad about it,' she said, 'but I can't tell you how relieved I am that he's dead. I would have shot him.'

'I'm glad you didn't have to.' He wondered if he'd ever tell her how grisly those moments were. He must have passed out at some point before the EMTs came. He didn't remember hearing the gunshot.

'It's over; finally it's all over,' Maureen said.

'Not quite,' Shanahan said.

Kowalski, who was standing in the doorway, came back in when Maureen went out for coffee. He hoped it would clear what was left of his brain.

'Why are you so sure Card is alive?' Kowalski asked. 'I saw two sets of prints, Shanahan.'

'So you say. Who would have killed him? Card created both sets by stepping back into his own prints. He made two trips. One around the house, then he backtracked, made a trip to the river, dropped some blood, sent the boat on its way and backtracked. Again. In the dim light of the morning and, if he was careful, you wouldn't have been able to see the double-step in the frost. By the time CSI got there and there was enough light to see the prints clearly, they were gone. The sun took care of the evidence.'

Despite its recent unpleasant history, Shanahan was glad to be home. But he wasn't prepared for what he saw when he got there. Standing in the living room just before the opening to the kitchen stood a dog. A large boxer, a fawn-colored specimen with a white chest, ears uncut and tail not bobbed. He looked at the approaching humans without fear. Though he barked, it was not threatening – more like a hello or, as it turned out, probably to advise the two men in the kitchen – Collins and Kowalski – of the homeowners' arrival.

Collins appeared in the doorway.

'This is Ray,' Collins said.

'Ray?' Shanahan asked involuntarily.

'As in "Sugar Ray,"' Collins said. 'The boxer.'

'Come on in,' Kowalski said. 'Make yourself at home.'

While Maureen and Ray got acquainted – she set him up with a water bowl – Shanahan found Kowalski bent over his laptop computer.

'You were holding out on me, Shanahan,' Collins said. 'Kowalski told me you are focusing on Thompkins.'

'And with good reason,' Kowalski said. 'She's on the board of Hunter's Bank.'

'Sounds about right for a very successful, highly ambitious business woman.'

'Sure,' Kowalski said, 'but that knowledge allowed us to put in other criteria and narrow the field: property sales, Hunter's Bank, Regina Thompkins, Indianapolis and Tyrus Investments. And now we have something.'

'What?' Maureen asked as Ray came up beside her and stood as if he was giving her away at the wedding. Father of the bride. Protector.

'Thompkins,' Kowalski said.

'I thought she helped you?' Collins said.

'By pointing us toward Daniel Holcomb,' Shanahan said.

'And you did a U-Turn?' Collins said, obviously unsatisfied.

Kowalski stood. 'My source said that Hunter's

Bank bought Tyrus Investments for forty million dollars.'

'So there was a Tyrus?' Shanahan asked. He looked at Collin. 'You see, Card *was* alive and there *was* a Tyrus.'

'Thank God you're not the kind of guy who likes to rub it in,' Collins said.

'Not exactly Tyrus,' Kowalski said. 'There was no real Tyrus. Nothing official, anyway. Just a folder with sheets of paper signed originally by the property owners and Judge Fournier. These, in turn, were signed over to Charles Bailey by his sister. Many of the options were already out of date. And the rest would run out soon. The whole package seemed worthless.'

'She gave them to Charles because they had little value,' Shanahan said. 'Charles didn't know about the key parcel, essential to a major development.'

'Your source?' Collins asked.

'Competing Bank,' said Kowalski. 'The word is that while there was a lot of junk in the package, mostly options, there was some land, not worth anything at the time and not part of Shanahan's dream Eastside development, land that the judge bought outright. One parcel was the land on which Second Chance was built and the land across the street. Both were deeded to the nonprofit. But there was a significant chunk south of Washington where serious redevelopment is going on. Hunter's wanted in on this. They needed the parcel that Fournier owned and options on adjacent parcels to build their own regional headquarters and all sorts of additional development. You know, something like "Hunter's Plaza." There were also a few spots on the Eastside, key locations for future branches.'

'And Mrs Thompkins fits in how?' Collins asked.

'Why don't we ask her?' Shanahan went to the cupboard. He pulled out a bottle of J.W. Dant Bourbon. 'I'll set up a time. You in, Kowalski?'

'Wouldn't miss it.'

Shanahan began to pour. 'Collins?'

'It's my party, isn't it? Better be, anyway.'

'Maureen?' Shanahan said. 'A rum and tonic for you?'

'Consider me one of the boys. A whiskey. I wouldn't miss it for the world.' She reached down to scratch Ray behind the ears. 'Can I bring a date?'

'Up to you and Ray. He's not my dog,' Collins said.

'You babysitting?' Shanahan said.

'Kind of,' he said. 'Ray's homeless.'

There was a long pause. 'Could we talk in the other room?'

They went into the living room.

'I don't know how to say this.'

'I have bad breath,' Shanahan said.

'Harold didn't kill Leonard Card.'

'He's alive?'

'No, you killed Card. Basically you crushed his windpipe before Harold shot him.'

'Oh.'

'Not a problem for us,' Collins said, 'but there's Harold and the records. Who knows what the media will dig up? Anyway, I'll tell Harold later.'

'Not a problem for me either.' Shanahan meant it. He had taken life before and, however despicable the victim was, killing someone was a big deal. But a flash of Nicky Hernandez's agonized face made this one go down easy. 'That all?'

'You're not easy to talk to . . .'

'And yet . . .?' Shanahan asked.

'I do.' Collins smiled. Direct approach. 'Will you take Ray?'

Shanahan knew there was a story behind Collins's watery eyes, but it looked painful and there was no reason to drag it out. 'Doesn't Ray have some say in this?'

'Not really. But, don't you think Maureen might?'

Collins followed Shanahan back to the kitchen.

'Ray needs a place to live,' Shanahan said, taking a sip of his whiskey.

'We've already talked about it,' Maureen said.

'What do you mean? Shanahan and I just . . .' Collins mumbled.

'She means she and Ray have already discussed it,' Shanahan said.

'And we've agreed,' she said. 'He gets room and board. In exchange, he has to take Shanahan out for a walk from time to time.' Maureen looked happy.

'My work is done,' Collins said, backing out of the kitchen, 'and a whole lot easier than I thought. Oh, I'll bring in some dog food. It's in in my trunk. Call me as soon as you know when we'll meet with the Thompkins lady.'

* * *

211

The neighborhood had recovered from the ice storm. At least, lights were on, though the ride home had been treacherous. Someone had put cardboard affixed with duct tape over the hole in the front window. He had things to do. Nails to remove, appointments to set up. He ran out of steam. Night came quickly.

Maureen fixed a quick pasta and sausage dinner. Ray, like all the dogs Shanahan had ever known, found his own sweet spot near the fireplace. Shanahan had as well, drifting in and out of consciousness until he woke long enough go to bed.

The bathroom called at three a.m. Ray made sure Shanahan got to his destination and back, quietly plodding behind him.

The old detective was awake before the sun. And very much awake. He made coffee, eggs and toast.

'Missing Cop Found' was the headline in the morning paper.

Missing Cop Found

Police have cautiously explained that IMPD officer Leonard Card had been involved in illicit undertakings, which are part of an ongoing investigation.

'We cannot comment on this at this time,' said Captain M.A. Collins, 'without jeopardizing a major case.' Collins did say that Card's death was a result of self-defense and that no one was being sought for his demise.

Anonymous sources within the police

department and confirmed by the district attorney indicate the investigation is connected to the sniper deaths of Alexandra Fournier and her brother, Charles Bailey.

'Are you famous yet?' Maureen asked as she came into the kitchen and saw the newspaper folded sloppily and pushed to the edge of the table.

The Thompkins lady was available at two. The conference room, on the top floor of a three-story branch of a gaudily lit Hunter's Bank branch, was made festive by gigantic, religion-free candy canes on the walls and contained a sixteen-seat, white marble-topped, oval conference table with all sixteen rolling chairs in red leather.

'It's pretty much Christmas all year long, I take it,' Kowalski said, looking around.

'I hope no one is diabetic,' Collins said.

Shanahan had made the appointment, telling her only that there were complications to do with some real estate transactions that involved her company and that's all he was at liberty to say. If she wanted to have an attorney present, she could.

When she demurred, Shanahan suggested the media might help him sort it out.

Captain Collins and James Fenimore Kowalski joined Shanahan and Maureen at one end of the long table. Jennifer Bailey sat at the other end, in almost a separate country. Harold stood behind her as if he were a Secret Service agent.

213

'Christmas already? Did I miss Thanksgiving?' Shanahan whispered to Maureen.

'Not yet,' she said. 'We still have time to miss it.'

Mrs Thompkins, having almost pulled off a classy holiday look – the dress was an emerald green rather than the brighter Christmas tone – came into the room wearing a cheery smile. She was followed by a slender, fashionably dressed young man with big, black-rimmed glasses.

Shanahan introduced everyone.

'This is Arthur, my attorney,' Thompkins said. He nodded.

'I hope it is not as serious as it sounds.' She sat, splitting the distance between Bailey and the others. Her attorney sat beside her. He pulled out a legal pad. 'What can I do for you?' she asked.

Shanahan introduced Maureen, Kowalski and Bailey. Thompins's pleasant but formal countenance disappeared when Captain Collins of the IMPD was introduced.

'How well did you know Leonard Card?' Shanahan asked her.

'As I told you earlier when we spoke about this, I interviewed him as part of my duties as a member of the police oversight committee.'

'Just once?'

'Yes, for about an hour.'

'Alone? Just the two of you?'

'Yes. To speed things up, perhaps you can tell me what this is all about,' she said, looking at her lawyer.

Collins leaned forward: 'Card knew the sniper who killed Alexandra Fournier and Charles

214

Bailey. Those two, aside from being sister and brother to Jennifer Bailey, were connected by a mysterious property investment group that might be extremely profitable for the current owner of those properties. The sniper is dead, suicide or homicide, we're not sure. And now Card is dead. He was someone who could explain what's going on. He died in an attempt to murder Mr Shanahan, who was closing in on this elusive Tyrus. Do you have any knowledge of Tyrus Investments?'

She looked at her attorney.

'All this talk of murder suggests to me that it would be in Miss Thompkins's best legal interest to answer no further questions until we know what this is all about,' said Arthur, the attorney.

'We're trying to find the person who issued the kill order,' Collins said as Thompkins and her attorney struggled to their feet.

'A good lawyer might want to know what we know and what we believe happened before having to deal with an arrest warrant,' Kowalski said.

This didn't stop the two.

'I'm sure Hunter's Bank will want to know what they're facing. You are on their board of directors, aren't you, Mrs Thompkins?' Kowalski continued.

'No questions,' her attorney said nervously.

'It's in the annual report,' Kowalski said, sliding a copy of the report down the table to him. 'Public record. In the President's letter there's talk of a fifty-story regional headquarters development south of Washington Street. Lots of land. A big investment.'

'It would take quite a group of powerful folks – people who know how to get things done – to put a real estate deal like that together,' Collins said.

Thompkins's attorney whispered something in her ear. She looked prepared to say something.

Kowalski interrupted. 'Is he your attorney or does he work for the bank?'

'We're done here,' she said firmly.

Jennifer Bailey pulled a cell phone out of her handbag. 'One call and I can have an army of forensic accountants down here to trace every transaction of Hunter's Bank for the last five years.'

'And you'll have nothing,' Thompkins said. But Arthur looked a little nervous. 'I have no idea why I am being questioned about any of this.'

'You tracked down the large, vital parcel of land that if not bought would prevent the Hunter dream from becoming real. You found the owner, who had signed an option agreement with the judge. The judge was dead. The trail went to Alexandra Fournier. You tracked her down and she explained she had turned them over to her brother. He had his eye on a scam of his own and you were able to buy the Hunter parcel cheap. And he was happy to keep everything secret, though you later worried about that.'

'Isn't it also interesting that Charles and everyone else who can tie you to the murders are dead?' Maureen asked.

'Don't make a fool of yourself, Maurie.'

'Funny you're the only one who ever called

me "Maurie,"' Maureen said with a slight grin. 'No one but you and Leonard Card.'

'Here are Card's last words to the world.' Shanahan walked around the table, handed Thompkins a copy of the note that had been tucked in Shanahan's morning paper. '"You and your lovely Maurie enjoy the last minutes of your lives."'

Thompkins looked away.

'He didn't know her name and even if he did he wouldn't have known to nickname her "Maurie,"' Shanahan said.

She looked back, visibly, honestly shaken.

'Why do you do this to me? I tried to help you,' Thompkins said.

'Amazing,' Kowalski said, standing. 'You lie. You steal. You kill. And *you* are the victim.'

Thompkins's lawyer cleared his throat. The world could hear him. 'That's all, folks.'

In the stunning quiet left behind by Thompkins's exit, Jennifer Bailey could be heard speaking into her cell phone. 'Brad,' she said, 'your office has jurisdiction here on part of this anyway. That's right. Hunter's Bank. By the way, are you sitting in my big old leather chair?' She laughed. 'That was a good investment of taxpayer money, then, wasn't it? Not what you said during the campaign, was it?' She laughed again. 'A Mrs Thompkins and who knows who else. Yes. Fraud. Murder. All sorts of juicy crimes,' she said. 'Not sure how much the bank knew. That's your job, but Thompkins's crimes are big time. She's a career-maker.'

'Tough as nails,' Kowalski said in a whisper.

'Check with Captain Collins at the IMPD,' Bailey said before putting her phone down.

'Perhaps you'll now have some time to recover,' she told Shanahan as she stood and prepared to leave.

'Yes, that would be nice,' Shanahan said. 'And you'll have time to grieve.'

'Who knows?' She almost smiled. 'Maybe you and Harold and I might need to work together again sometime.'

Twenty-Eight

Dinner was over. Snow fell. Large flakes were visible through the new pane of glass in the living-room window. Shanahan and Kowalski, each with a glass of whiskey, sat in the upholstered chairs that occupied space on either side of the fireplace. Ray and Maureen owned the sofa.

'Ray should have a cigar,' Kowalski said.

'Ray's smarter than that. Look how fit he is. And he's middle-aged,' Maureen said. 'A little gray on the muzzle.'

'I was enjoying the meal so much I forgot to tell you,' Kowalski said. 'Thompkins hired Holcomb to defend her.'

'The videotape?' Maureen asked. 'It implicated Holcomb.'

'That's where Thompkins's skill at manipulation truly shines,' Kowalski said. 'Well, briefly. She rearranged everything: facial expressions, comments out of order and in a creative way to tell the story she wanted to tell to support your suspicions, Shanahan. She edited the tape,' Kowalski went on. 'Inventive. Convincing.'

'How did you know?' Maureen asked. She sipped her spiked eggnog.

'Holcomb wore this oversized, expensive analog watch. Looking closely, time wasn't only going forward but backward, then forward, then backward again. She almost pulled it off. They still don't have her signature on anything.'

'She'll be running the prison,' Shanahan said.

'When did you know it was Thompkins?' Kowalski asked Shanahan.

'I didn't, until the note. I wondered why Holcomb would get involved. He had all the money he needed. Trust-fund baby and a thriving practice. He wanted the spotlight. And that was guaranteed. All he had to do was not screw it up. Then there was Jennifer Bailey and her trusted bodyguard.'

'Really, with all the two of you have been through over the years? You think she'd kill her sister and brother?'

'Her sister stole her boyfriend, the judge, who had property worth more than even he ever imagined. And Jennifer's no-good brother ran off with it. I wouldn't cross her. Turned out it was another tough woman, this one operating out of pure greed.'

'And the sniper?' Maureen said. 'Another tough woman?'

'Maybe she couldn't cope with being locked up for the rest of her life. Maybe she loved and couldn't stand the idea of life without him.'

'Hard to imagine. Maybe he had her killed rather than risk her testimony.'

Shanahan shook his head. 'I don't know how we will ever find out now. The players are dead.'

'No mystery is ever solved completely,' Maureen said.

Shanahan had some unresolved questions as well. Who killed Leonard Card? Collins made sure Card's official killer was Shanahan in self-defense. Had it been Harold, the retired state trooper might face formal inquiries. No matter what Shanahan came to believe, he would always have some doubt.

The best to come from this was that the most culpable got what they deserved. Card was dead. Samantha would kill no one else. Thompkins, who orchestrated it all, was found out. And she was going to pay.

Kowalski left, his low-growling Harley violating the silent snow. Maureen kissed Shanahan on the forehead, familiar with the nightly routine. He would sit for a while before making the security rounds. Ray followed Maureen to the bedroom, but must have returned. When Shanahan woke again, Ray was at his feet. The fire, a glowing piece of log, no longer lit the room.

'I was thinking of a Belgian Shepherd,' Shanahan said to the dog. 'One hundred fifty pounds, police trained. But I think you'll do just fine. You'll take good care of her, won't you?'